Welcome to the Seventh Spark Universe

Prepare for the most immersive novel you have ever experienced. Eye-popping visuals, intriguing dialogue, and a captivating story that whisks you away to world where the physical and spiritual realms intertwine in an epic story of good versus evil... Enjoy!

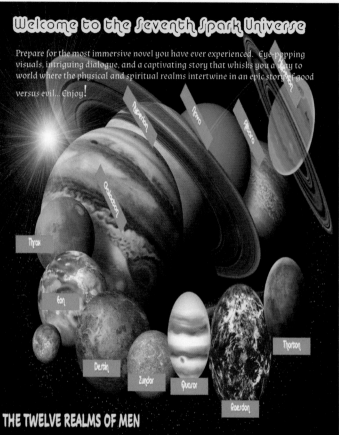

THE TWELVE REALMS OF MEN

Our Team

J.B LION
Writer & Creative Director
www.jblion.com

T.D. SHANNON
Editor

MIKE D
Illustrator

Rebecca Brewer
Chief Editor
https://reedsy.com/rebecca-brewer

KNIGHTS OF THE TRINITY
Volume One of the Seventh Spark Series

Creative Writers Group

Publisher's Note: This is a work of fiction. Names, characters, places, and incidents are a product of the author's imagination. Locales and public names are sometimes used for atmospheric purposes. Any resemblance to actual people, living or dead, or to businesses, companies, events, institutions, or locales is completely coincidental.

Seventh Spark – Knights of the Trinity / J.B. Lion -- 1st ed.
ISBN: 978-1-7351534-0-7

The Seventh Spark

An Immersive Reading Experience

Dear Reader,

It is with great pride that I present my work to you as an offering of entertainment and distraction from the drudgery of the everyday grind. As a business professional for over 20 years, I know the stress and toll it takes on your mental, physical, and spiritual body to get up to a job you hate, support a household that unknowingly overlooks your sacrifice, and live in a world that continually censors ability to truly express yourself under the vale of free speech and equality for all. To people who can relate to this, I wrote this for you. My objective as a writer is to write stories that challenge the socio-economic, spiritual, and racial barriers that have stood for centuries; to make my readers think about why they believe what they believe. In this, we gain perspective, and through perspective, we build tolerance. Writing this book series was truly a labor of love. I hope you enjoy reading it as much as I enjoyed bringing it to life.

As for the story itself

The Seventh Spark Series will make you laugh, cry, scream, but most-importantly., it will challenge you on an intellectual, social, and spiritual level. Enjoy! ☺

"I can do all things through Christ who strengthens me."

Phillippians 4:13

EPISODES CONTAINED IN THIS VOLUME — KNIGHTS OF THE TRINITY

1 Darkness Falls

"I AM SAVING MAN, FROM THEMSELVES" – The Reaper

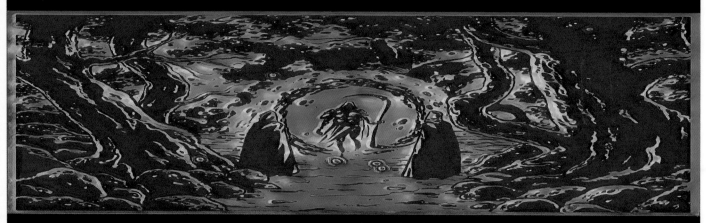

In the darkness of night, few things could be darker. The sky covered the earth in a thick blanket of gloom, two figures stood, one next to the other, posturing cloaked in hooded garments which competed with the murkiness of the night for attention. Their eyes stretched out over the desolate land. It was overrun by dead brush; the hanging limbs of tree branches swayed violently, slapping them in the face as they continued their march forward. The wind howled, a biting chill, determined to punish the dark souls for lingering where they did not belong. Even the sky appeared cursed; one sole star engulfed by the shadows of darkness; the celestial body would act as their guide, leading them, tormenting them. Yet fear and anguish were not foreign to these lowly beings; they welcomed the terrors of the night. Damnation marked them, wretched souls, who reveled in mischief and mayhem. One began to pace, uneasy with anticipation.

Can you stop?" the unmoving companion requested.

"The meta-anthropoid is belated, his presence overdue," the other figure muttered.

"What?"

"It is past the witching hour; I expected better from the inaugurator of this devious machination."

"Your constant jittering won't make him come any faster, one eye," the other said in a menacing tone.

"Keen observation nefarious figure. I am an assuredly exceptional being, unbeknown to likes of your genus. Allow me to demonstrate."

REMOVING THE HOODED CLOAK WHICH CONCEALED IT, ILLUMINATED THE VIOLET SPLENDOR OF HIS AURA. A CELESTIAL BEING BORN FROM THE UNIVERSE ITSELF; A GLOWING BRILLIANCE, A GODLY SIGHT NOT MEANT FOR THE EYES OF MAN. A SINGULAR ORB CENTERED IN THE MIDDLE OF HIS ARROW-LIKE CRANIUM, A CYCLOPTIC GAZE,

YELLOW IRIS, RED PUPIL.

His companion was not impressed. Becoming increasingly impatient with how much his adversary seemed to be so impressed with himself, he could no longer resist the urge to respond in-kind.

"You are peculiar, little one, but I have seen stranger things than alien princes. I have existed since the great divide thousands of years ago, before planets and stars." the mysterious figure explained while removing his hood.

The prince gazed in amazement. This was no man nor alien; this was a being from the spirit world, a world long forgotten by the alien lord.

ITS FIGURE WAS VERY THE DEFINITION OF EVIL ITSELF. THE COLOR OF MIDNIGHT, JET BLACK SLENDER YET FIRM FRAME, COVERED IN ANCIENT MARKINGS AND SPELLS; NO DOUBT FROM THE DEPTHS OF WHERE IT CAME FROM. BUT THE WORST GREW INSIDE OF IT. SIX HEADS, SIX FACES, SIX DAMNED SOULS ENCASED AND TRAPPED INSIDE A SEEMINGLY OTHERWISE FRAGILE FRAME. SERRATED TEETH PROTRUDING OUT OF EACH ONE, CHOPPING, BITING, HOWLING...MOVING. A DEVILISH SIGHT, SOME GREAT SPELLS HELD THESE CREATURES AT BAY, GIVING THEIR MASTER POWER.

A chill ran up the spine of the alien prince, although he would never admit to his terror; the look of disgust was telling enough to bring a sly grin to the ancient demon's face. The prince was so distracted by the ill sight, it did not notice that the gyrating branches of the crooked trees had come to a halted salute. A portal from another realm had been opened. The guest of honor had arrived.

"Patience is a virtue. But of course, I won't

expect savages like you to understand that."

His voice was forbidding, thundering even, but it did not deter the two who had waited a long time for him.

"Late in the hour, this Magellan decides to arrive. Yet he affronts us!" the prince exclaimed. "I should convoke my horde to rip out your throat and feast on your flesh."

"Ah, I see you understand the language, Kreetus. Impressive. The intelligence of your race was not exaggerated. But I need you and your millions of soldiers for their legendary savagery, not for their mastery of the common tongue. Remember, your presence here is because I will it. If you threaten me again, we will see how well you speak with your head sliced from your shoulders. The mysterious figure glared hard at the prince of the Trarkards. Never forget that it was I who gave you and your race a second chance at survival."

Kreetus's royal velvet glow began to morph heated crimson as he battled with fury to nod in the submission of his full compliance. He knew better than to allow his rage to show. It was more of a risk to his kind, especially with them being nearer to extinction. Allegiance was his for now. It was a far more reasonable course to take than to display his disgust and be doomed to inevitable destruction.

Legion stood by, letting out a chuckle, an audience to this witless banter, wondering how much more time they would waste at odds. While he was off his guard and entertained by the amusing scene playing out before him, one of his demons confined within, attempted to make an escape. Nearly emancipated before Legion grabbed hold and forcefully thrust him back in-side. The moment of merriment was quickly depleted, replaced by the exasperation of betrayal.

"Disgusting," Reaper spat, turning to look at Legion disapprovingly. *"Seems you're losing control of them."*

"My children are hungry. "They need to eat,"

"Don't worry about them," Legion said as all six faces pulled away from his body, giving it a grotesque shape. *"They belong to me and are mine to control."*

The faces hissed and quickly snapped back into the demon's body. The Reaper looked on in contempt.

"Now, let's get down to business," the Reaper said, clasping his hands together with his scythe.

The two with him turned to him with the most rapt attention.

"After many centuries of patiently waiting, the realm of men is finally about to fall.

The seventh spark has been lit for the ten realms; only planets Eon and Thorton remain protected. That was until yesterday. Atrocities from a civil war in Thorton has wrought the lighting of the seventh spark for their realm. Now only Planet Eon remains."

He paused and stared at the two in front of them. *"That is where you two come into play."*

Legion decided to ask what they both were thinking, *"What is a spark, and why are seven of them so important?"*

The Reaper wasted no time explaining, *"A spark is exactly what it means. An igniting of something that spreads, and soon it becomes difficult to contain. The sparks, in this case, represent sin, not just any sin, a major undertaking of evil that spreads and infects life, changing the way humans live forever."*

" The Everlasting protects the fall of man for six of these catastrophes, but once there is a seventh, well... anything goes"

The two nodded their understanding.

"Legion, you will go to Thorton to prepare the planet for Kreetus and the Horde's invasion. Bring the chaos, fear, and pain you're legendary for. The men on this planet are in the middle of a civil war. They are dripping with sin; this should be easy for you. After that, you can begin wreaking havoc on Eon."

"As you wish," Legion replied, bowing comically, drool falling from his mouth. *"But what about the Twelve? Won't one of them be there on Thorton waiting for me? One of the precious Knights of the Trinity? The Everlasting's chosen warriors, who banished me so long ago? I have heard about the one they call Demons' Bane."*

THE REAPER

"A SPARK IS EXACTLY WHAT IT MEANS. AN IGNITING OF SOMETHING THAT SPREADS AND SOON IT BECOMES DIFFICULT TO CONTAIN. THE SPARKS, IN THIS CASE, REPRESENT SIN, NOT JUST ANY SIN, A MAJOR UNDERTAKING OF EVIL THAT SPREADS AN INFECTS LIFE, CHANGING THE WAY HUMANS LIVE FOREVER."

I am told he is not one to be trifled with. He should be a good fight for us." "Oh, how I miss the blood of an angel on the edge of my mighty battle-ax!"

"Yes," the Reaper said, quickly turning away to shield his turn of emotion, which had suddenly settled on his face. "Do what you must. As much as it pains me, the time of the Everlasting Order has ended." The sulk in his shoulders deepened as the words he spoke began to hit home.

"Time for my ax to get another trophy," Legion smirked, throwing his ax into

the air and snatching it from there. "Are you finished?!" the Reaper exploded. "Just do what you are told to do so we can get this over with!"

"Aye, captain," Legion replied, a smile of mockery in his face. "I know this must be hard for you, turning to the dark si…"

The devil's words halted deep within his throat and became muffled as the Reaper's fingers closed in around it with an iron grip, which tightened with every passing moment. His legs hung limp as his body became a heap of stones bearing down on them. He had come to the realization of what was happening. Death was a promise which he planned to fight, even as life begged to find the release of slipping away within him.

The rapid pace of events caught the alien prince off guard. He rushed forward to provide aid and stop this madness, raising his sword to attack; the blade of its weapon emblazed with heat, illuminating Kreetus's every step.

The Reaper was in a mood to be distracted. While he clutched the gullet of Legion, and with his free extension, he hoisted Kreetus high into the air. The sword the prince gripped came crashing down with a loud thud. The prince's violet hue turned red, its struggle for life now matched its companion.

"Let me make something clear to you, lowly filths!" The Reaper began. "I detest evil; I detest looking at your ugly faces. Darkness can never triumph over light unless it is ALLOWED to! Remember this, and you might just get to keep your pitiful lives a while longer. I'm not destroying man; I'm saving man from themselves."

Guardians of the Realm

"All Hail Artemus, The Protector" - Knights of the Everlasting Order

Thunder roared. Lightning flashed. The skies erupted from the vibrations of clashing adversaries. Continuous pops of explosions boomed for all to hear, yet the visuals of the confrontation concealed, hidden by some dark magic. Two combatants of an ancient age locked in a furious battle that lasted days.

Time was a trifle to these immortals. Death was the only means to an end. A mountain of a man, ten feet tall, the

expanse of his muscles poured over his body, yielding half the width of his height. His legs and arms thick as tree trunks interlocked with a creature, lean and lanky with skin as dark as midnight. Thick golden armor adorned a broad chest with the craftsman-ship of Hephaestus while his adversary fought naked, gnarled, and nasty; demonic faces with serrated teeth protruding from his slender frame.

Eyes locked as heavy rains pounded the ground beneath them. Lightning cracked the sky, striking a tree and igniting a flame.

The prodigious figure took advantage of the distraction.

Blinding white light illuminated from its aura. The creatures' knee buckled under the mighty force of the being's strength. The saturated ground gave quickly, trapping the once nimble monster in the mud and muck. The illuminated entity acted fast. With both hands above its head and it came down hard on its enemy with

massive force. The planet shook every time it pounded the creature deeper and deeper into the ground until not a hair on its head could be seen from the naked eye. One more blow for good measure. Now was not the time to show mercy. Deeper and deeper into the planet's core, or the depths of hell. No cries of anguish or sorrow were made, not even a whimper. Perhaps the creature lacked the wits to speak, or the words beat out of it. It mattered not.

Only the total eradication of its very being held meaning. To ponder on such things in the heat of battle was folly. The focus was on the imminent victory; however, the spiraling pull of a dragging defeat began to bubble up in the pit of his stomach. His shoulders lifted, the first approach at resistance to the pull, and his whole body soon followed suit. This promised victory, and the time he took to boast from within, had drawn him closer to morbidity than he had even considered. Could he be sinking as well?

HE WAS SINKING. PROLONGED SKELETAL HANDS OF FIRE CLUTCHED THE BASE OF HIS FEET. NOT ONE, NOT TWO, BUT WHAT APPEARED TO BE HUNDREDS. NO DOUBT, A PLOT CARRIED OUT TO PERFECTION BY HIS ADVERSARY.

GLOOM, HELD CAPTIVE IN THE ATMOSPHERE, PERMEATING THE MOOD WITH A MORBID EMBRACE SEIZING ALL OF HIM. THE GLOWING FIGURE WAS SINKING AND SINKING FAST. THE EON SHOOK ONCE AGAIN. OUT OF THE MUCK AND MIRE ROSE A NEMESIS WHO WAS NO STRANGER.

DRAPED HEAD TO TOE IN ITS FILTHINESS, THE DEAD HAD ARISEN, READY TO DO BATTLE ONCE MORE. THIS TIME, IT BROUGHT SOMETHING FROM THE UNDERWORLD WITH IT. THE BEING CLUTCHED A LONG BATTLE-AXE WITH STRANGE MARKINGS ON ITS HILT. CURSED SPIRITS WITH FACES OF ANGUISH LITTERED ITS DOUBLE-SIDED BLADE. THE MOANS FROM THEIR DESPAIR SEEMED TO GIVE THE WEAPON SOME ACCURSED ENCHANTMENT.

THE TOWERING FIGURE OPPOSING IT DID NOT CARE TO FIND OUT.

THE MIGHTY SPECIMEN STRUGGLED FREE FROM THE CLUTCHES OF THE DEMONIC HANDS BELOW AND REESTABLISHED SURE FOOTING. BOTH MOVED IN AND OUT OF ATTACKS, QUICKLY BRINGING DEADLY FORCE BEHIND EVERY BLOW. THEY DANCED AS IF CONDUCTING A SYMPHONY, EVERY MOVE CALCULATED, STRATEGIC, DEADLY; THE BATTLE REACHED ITS CRESCENDO.

WITH HIS LEFT AND RIGHT HAND, THE MAMMOTH FIGURE RIPPED OUT TWO FORTY-FOOT CEDARLIS TREES FROM THE WET GROUND AND HURLED THEM WITH A FURY OF SAMPSON. THE HERCULEAN FEAT WAS NOT TO BE OUTDONE BY ITS ADVERSARY'S AGILITY AND WIT. IT ELUDED THE FIRST TREE, THEN NIMBLY JUMPED ONTO THE SECOND ONE. ANOTHER GRACEFUL LEAP INTO THE AIR; BATTLE-AXE COCKED AND READY TO STRIKE.

THE EDGE OF THE BLADE SPLIT THE MASSIVE FIGURE INTO TWO PIECES WITH PERFECT PRECISION. THE BODY HIT THE GROUND WITH AN ENORMOUS THUD AS IT BEGAN TO SINK INTO THE MURKY BUBBLING SLUSH BELOW. THE CREATURE ROARED IN VICTORY AS DID THE FORCES OF HELL IN-SIDE OF HIM. IT RAISED ITS AXE HIGH IN DELIGHT. A HUSHED PRAYER OR SPELL PUSHED PAST ITS LIPS. HIS GREAT AXE BEGAN TO GLOW FIERY RED. THE FALLEN WARRIOR'S DEATH WAS JUST THE BEGINNING OF HIS SACRIFICE TO PROTECT THE REALM HE LOVED.…

Diffused golden light cast its soft illumination beneath a rain-bow sky that arced over a lush landscape of plush white clouds. A gate of brightest gold with ancient runes etched in gleaming pearl guarded the entrance to the heavenly realm, an effective barrier against those who did not belong; those who were not worthy of stepping foot into the pristine oasis. Echoing the aurora borealis of the sky, an enormous rainbow arched over the realm, its perfect shape, and distinct colors reminding all who received permission to enter God's infinite mercy. Walking through the golden gates, the visitor eventually came to an arc standing beside a rock from which sparkling waves of crystal water flowed.

At once ponderous and graceful, a visitor who dared touch the mighty arc felt the inflexible rigidity of stone instead of the penetrable, lively timber of wood beneath his fingers. The material of construction spoke not of sailing open waters, but of another purpose. The arc served as a high table around which only the greatest and noblest of beings could gather. All who desired a seat eagerly awaited an invitation to the high calling of being a guest to the Supreme Being.

Armin, the Divine, wisest of his brethren, sat at the head of that celestial arc. Attired in a glittering silk cloak and elegant cere-monial garb appropriate to the solemn occasion. The sophisticated curve of their every muscle shadowed his wafer-like build.

The Seventh Spark – Knights of the Trinity

Despite his slight stature, none of his brothers made a mistake-- at least not more than once--of doubting his prowess as a warrior and strategist. Fierce as each of his brothers was, none matched him in lethal skill. They deferred to him because he was someone who garnered and demanded their everlasting respect.

A flash of white light speared through the golden haze of that holy realm to slam with soundless authority upon the surface of the high table. It blinked for a moment then vanished, leaving behind an ancient book smelling of dust and its parchment pages opened to number 3,107. A quill pen lay on the open page, its tip fresh and sharp and yet unstained by the permanent ink that would soon flow at the command of the one who wielded it. Armin, the Divine, took the pen in his pale, thin hand, filled his lungs with the tingling purity of that realm's air, and summoned his brothers

to initiate the day's ceremony.

 The three thousand one hundred seventh meeting of the Knights of the Trinity has come to order. Roll call."

"Stevyn the Beast is here, and Rupin, of course," came the first booming reply from the next eldest brother.

With skin tanned as though deeply burnished by constant exposure to the sun, Stevyn materialized at Armin's right hand. White rhinoceros hide draped over his shoulders, thighs, and arms. A long staff hung on his back, nearly lost amid the long, thick dreadlocks that he dared not cut dangled to those trunk-like thighs. Ancient runes engraved the skin of his face and chiseled chest. Stevyn claimed the runes protected him from evil. Beside him, a tremendous saber-toothed cat growled its bestial warning before settling comfortably beside its master.

Saliva dripped from the long fangs into the fluffy clouds upon which they stood.

 "Must you always bring that mangy beast? Her musk is overpowering" Armin muttered with distaste.

Stevyn grinned at him; his teeth filed to sharp points. *"Rupin goes where I go."*

 "The Conqueror returns home, brothers!" the next brother announced himself. "Anyone want to challenge me? I'm in the mood for a good scrap."

Armin pinched the bridge of his nose at Gaudfridus' unwarranted cheer. Shorter than all his brothers, he made up for his lack of height with a breadth that generated awe and terror. The defiant gleam of his golden armor and the massive battle-ax slung behind his shoulders helped solidify that impression. Gaudfridus did not come by the sobriquet "The Conqueror" without good reason.

 "Hey, you, old gargoyle, any day, any time,"

"Now is not the time, Gaudfridus" Armin chided his irrepressible, gray-skinned brother.

With uncharacteristic meekness, the mighty warrior simply nodded and held his tongue.

Armin's nose twitched as he sensed the presence of another of his brethren and said,

 "Jewel, is that you?"

"Jewel, la ponopia de gremilaze, es redaomas,"

 "Jewel, we all agreed to speak English this millennium. I have reminded you of this at least a hundred times by now" Armin reminded his youngest sibling.

Light, lilting, sharp as the keenest razor, his sister's voice floated through the illuminated air:

"Okay, okay. The Valiant one it here."

"More like the defiant one."

Armin whispered under his breath as his brothers snickered. Even that awful cat seemed to find unholy amusement in his irritation. He contemplated kicking the animal but did not want to offend Stevyn, who held the beast utmost in his affections.

"I heard that"

Jewel said as she manifested and gave him an unrepentant grin that cut more keenly than any of her blades ever did. Standing a litter taller and equally as slender as Armin, her brilliant green eyes glowed from beneath a platinum helm boasting a gleaming blue sapphire centered like a third eye. Glittering and strangely malleable, her sapphire armor did not clink or restrict her movement in any way. Her long, white hair flowed from beneath

the helmet to cascade like a moonlight waterfall between the two samurai swords strapped to her back.

Armin fought the urge to flick his fingers at his youngest sibling's platinum helm, a gesture as much of annoyance as affection. She'd slice off his fingers before he could react.

 "Anisau"

Armin the Divine summoned in ringing tones, waiting with stoic patience his third and most mischievous brother's appearance.

"I'm here. No, I'm over here. Now, here I am again."

Armin pinched the bridge of his nose again.

 *"Cease your infernal running, Anisau, and standstill"*

Anisau the Swift obeyed, screeching to halt between his oldest and youngest siblings.

 "I never saw you"

"Your eyes betray you lovely, I was here the whole time." *"I know, you've circled the arc seven thousand seven hundred fifty-two times now. Please hold still."*

Gaudfridus shook his head and muttered,

"Don't you have anything better to do?"

Stevyn looked at Armin in amazement,

"Unbelievable! How did you know he was here?"

"You underestimate me brother. I might not have vision like Reimund, but I can see Anisau, even when he's running like a fool."

Anisau's brilliant white teeth gleamed behind a sizable oval mask made of alligator skin and lined with elephant hide, Anisau read the

ancient runes on the interior of the veil that only he could see. His ebony skin gleamed, stretched tautly over a lean runner's frame that topped the rest of his siblings. Other than the mask, he wore the only loincloth for modesty. Anything else impeded his movement.

"You ready to take off that mask yet? After eight-hundred and eighty-eight years, don't you think it is time? I can't imagine what that thing smells like," Gaudfridus asked, curious as to where all the siblings as to what their brother looked like behind the mask he never ever removed.

"Nah, he's scared his ugly face will give us nightmares,"

"Ha! Quite the opposite, sis. I'm scared my beauty will bring the rest of you despair and into depression."

Behind the mask, he raised an eyebrow in challenge.

"You could always try to take it off me... Again."

"Once was enough. Hell, I've still got a stitch in my side from trying to catch you the last time."

"You got off easy, I tore my hamstring chasing after that little bastard."

Anisau chuckled and wagged his finger.

"Sticks and Stones. Truth is none of you will EVER catch me."

Armin sighed and glowered at his brother in wordless command to stay put and quit antagonizing his siblings. Anisau's mask dipped slightly in a small nod of acquiescence.

The joyous recollection of times past took an abrupt turn as Berlot, materialized to join his brethren.

"The White Wolf is here," he paused in dismay as he noticed the figure to the left of him, barely within his gaze.

"Oh, I see you made it, Stevyn. I didn't realize they still allowed cheaters into the Third Realm."

Good Lord, not again, Armin thought to himself. He would have to act fast to keep the peace.

"Cheater?" Stevyn snorted. "Why dear brother, are you still upset that my scout Hazel bested your Zachariah?"

"Bested?" Berlot took offense, "Bested, you say?" "Well, I guess when your set traps in the Oracle before the fight, you can say whatever you wish. I should have taken your head for the offense."

"Well, I am standing right here, little brother. I can still best you. Have you forgotten?"

"Don't call me that! Never call me that! We are twins, I am not your little brother."

"Aww, yes, young one, but who materialized first? All your life, you have tried to one-up me, and still you fail. Do you want a hug, little brother?"

IN AN INSTANT, THE TWO RUSHED AT EACH OTHER WITH MURDEROUS INTENT. STEVYN, RUPIN EVER BY HIS SIDE, HURLED HIS LONG SPEAR, AN IMPOSSIBLE THROW, AIMED DEAD CENTER TO THE CHEST OF THE SLIGHTLY BROADER BERLOT. WITS ABOUT HIM, BERLOT TRANSFORMED INTO HIS MAJESTIC WHITE WOLF, GLOWING RED EYES, SHARP FANGS, AND CLAWS. HE LEAPED AT HIS PREY. THE TWO MET IN MID-AIR. RUPIN, STEVYN'S PROTECTOR, AND THE WHITE WOLF, SIZE DWARFING THAT OF THE PREHISTORIC CAT. RUPIN WHIMPERED IN PAIN, DOING ITS BEST TO DEFEND AGAINST THE MORE IMPOSING AND FASTER ADVERSARY. STEVYN COULD ONLY WATCH AS HE FIDDLED WITH HIS LEATHER SATCHEL DESPERATELY SEARCHING FOR HIS HUNTING KNIFE.

"Stop this madness at once!" Armin shouted at the top of his lungs with a verbosity he was not known for. It did the trick.

"Berlot, return to your angelic form, I will not ask a second time!"

Like a good soldier, Berlot obeyed his leader's command.

Stevyn was not as obedient.

"Look, what you did to my Rupin!" "You could have killed her!"

Berlot did not say a word; he just gave a slight nod of the head and a sly smirk to agree with his brother's assessment.

Armin piped up,

"Stevyn, I said no more!" You started this mess and look what happened. Rupin had to pay the price for your arrogance. You two have been at this for seventy years now. Enough! Shake hands, and that is the end of it."

Reluctantly, the two fraternal brothers complied with Armin's not so subtle request.

Stevyn, a tear in his eye, quickly turned to check on his faithful companion Rupin, a large gash running from her neck to her belly. Gaudfridus gave him a slight pat on the back for comfort

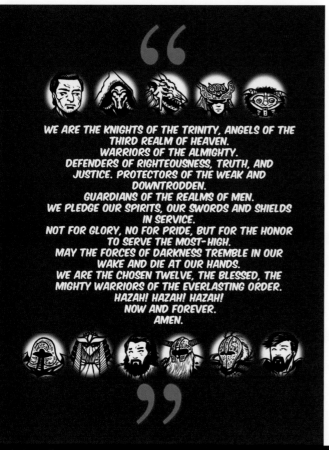

WE ARE THE KNIGHTS OF THE TRINITY, ANGELS OF THE
THIRD REALM OF HEAVEN.
WARRIORS OF THE ALMIGHTY.
DEFENDERS OF RIGHTEOUSNESS, TRUTH, AND
JUSTICE. PROTECTORS OF THE WEAK AND
DOWNTRODDEN.
GUARDIANS OF THE REALMS OF MEN.
WE PLEDGE OUR SPIRITS, OUR SWORDS AND SHIELDS
IN SERVICE.
NOT FOR GLORY, NO FOR PRIDE, BUT FOR THE HONOR
TO SERVE THE MOST-HIGH.
MAY THE FORCES OF DARKNESS TREMBLE IN OUR
WAKE AND DIE AT OUR HANDS.
WE ARE THE CHOSEN TWELVE, THE BLESSED, THE
MIGHTY WARRIORS OF THE EVERLASTING ORDER.
HAZAH! HAZAH! HAZAH!
NOW AND FOREVER.
AMEN.

"What is the tear for? You have dominion over animals, just heal the damn cat, like you've done a thousand times before, and be done with it."

"It is the principal of the matter. Berlot should have never attacked her like that."

"And you should have never antagonized your brother like that! Do you want to keep playing the blame game? Or would you rather drink some ale I brought back from Zundor? This has got to be the best batch I have ever made."

The twinkle of a grin sparked in his eyes. Slowly he allowed the cheer to spread to his lips, forming a full 'Cheshire cat' veneer and displaying all his teeth. He was no longer bothered, and the ale was a peace offering.

He knelt to say a prayer over Rupin. The moment the last word was uttered, Rupin was as good as new, purring in satisfaction from the rubdown he received from the hands of his master.

In all the excitement, Armin failed to realize the rest of the Order had arrived, and none too soon. He summoned each one of them by name: Lucis, Greggarious, Raj, Berlot, Zane. Each materialized as Armin gave his name voice until ten brothers and one sister gathered around the impressive table, the absence of one brother conspicuous.

With a nod of acknowledgment at the full gathering of his family, Armin raised his arms and intoned,

"Brothers in arms, we are gathered here to honor Artemus who gave his spirit to protect Planet Thorton from demonic forces. Let us honor him by reciting our pledge."

Together they recited in mournful chorus:

Stevyn "the Beast"
Protector of Quasor
Blessing: DOMINION OVER ANIMALS

Gaudfridus "The Conqueror"
Protector of Zundor
Blessing: FURY OF GOD

Jewel "The Valiant"
Protector of Nova
Blessing: VOICE OF GOD

Ansiau "the Swift"
Protector of Thrax
Blessing: SPEED OF GOD

Raj "The Ancient"
Protector of Raesdon
Blessing: WRATH OF GOD

Reimund "The Hunter"
Protector of Galacton
Blessing SIGHT OF GOD

Lucis "the Lightbringer"
Protector of Earth(Eon)
Blessing: LIGHT OF GOD

Berlot "The White Wolf"
Protector of Destin
Blessing: SPIRIT OF GOD

Artemus "The Protector"
Protector of Thorton
Blessing: STRENGHT OF GOD

Zane "The Vigilant"
Protector of Hyperion
Blessing: PATIENCE OF GOD

Azrael "The Magnificent"
Protector of Nyperion
Blessing: MIND OF GOD

Armin" The Wise"
Protector of Altara
Blessing: BREATH OF GOD

Absolution "Demon's Bane"
Michael's Protector
(not an order member)

Michael the Archangel
Protector of all Realms; creator of the Everlasting Order

THE EVERLASTING ORDER

"Please, be seated," Armin said. Looking over his brethren, he continued,

"Artemus, the Protector, sacrificed his life in service to our Lord. It is a tradition that we dine on the food and drink of his realm to honor him."

"Why haven't we amended that part of the articles, the food from Thorton is terrible"

Lucis muttered under his breath in distaste, his gleaming white wings ruffling.

Taking his seat, Armin directed a reproving glare at him.

 "It's tradition and tradition we must obey. Now, let the feast begin!"

White light flashed again, making Lucis's pale blue skin glow and leaving behind silver goblets filled to their brims with fizzing, blue liquid.

"What is this ilk?"

Greggarious the Hunter barked, wrinkling his nose. He shifted in his chair and fanned the steam rising from the hot blue liquid.

"Only the most popular drink in Thorton. Deikrj! Let's drink."

As one, they raised their goblets and drank.

Greggarious gagged. Blue liquid spewed from his nose, the vile odor, and taste overpowering his ability to choke down the fluid.

"This is just awful. I forgot how disgusting the ale is in Thorton." He shook his head and wiped his face with his sleeve. *"Terrible"*

Jewel frowned at his poor table manners.

"Greggarious, nice fur" "Is that your latest kill?"

Greggarious stroked the black bearskin draped over his shoulders and down his back. The gleaming fur contrasted sharply with his orange skin. He leaned his lanky body back in the chair and pulled out a golden arrow which he set on the table.

 "Indeed. I killed the beast with this arrow."

"And how many others?"

Arching one side of his unibrow, Greggarious's upper lip lifted in a sneer.

 "Ha! Good one, Galdy! Just the one, as always. I never miss."

"Well, I would hope so, Greg" "I mean, you are blessed with the sight of the Almighty" "Hey green eyes, how's the ale?"

Jewel set down her empty cup and grimaced.

"I am choking it down. I need something to take the edge off being around you jerks all day. I prefer the beer of the Earth realm. Actually, I would prefer my own bile to this muck."

"Have you tried the ginger ale on Planet Nyperion? I thought that was horrid, but this fizzy blue sludge might just change my mind." "What do you think, Raj, you old buzzard."

Raj took a sip and let the liquid linger on his tongue before swallowing.

"Hmm...not bad. It just needs a touch of hornsilk from Raesdon in Realm Seven, and it would be just right."

 "Why ask Raj?" "He will find the silver lining inside a glub-infested tar pit,"

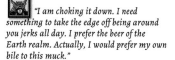

This is a glub

 "I think he's been taking too many of his own mediation tonics. We all know how awful those are. He's killed his own taste buds."

Raj the Ancient One ignored them and tipped the goblet into his beak, his taloned hand gripping the stem of the cup with impressive dexterity. More bird than man, he extended his feathered wings behind him, then furled them again a move purposely made to peacock the grandeur of color and size from his wingspan. The vibrant color burnished the gold of his armor and the violet of his skin, making them appear in perfect unison. The black talons of his right hand tightened over the jewel-encrusted scepter he always carried and which he claimed gave him the power to unleash the chaos tightly contained within him.

Berlot frowned and sniffed at the remaining contents of his goblet. Making a face, he said,

 "No way. Give me some scorndle from Destin, and I'm good."

Raj shrugged, ignoring his shape-shifting brother, who favored the formation of a white wolf. He glared at his brethren

and sighed with disappointment.

"WHEW, man that is foul. My nose is on fire! Must you always wear those musty old animal skins?"

 "Wow, that is the most animated I have ever seen, Raj. Congrats, Berlot. Your stench has broken him."

Berlot stroked the thick albino wolf's pelt he wore, the beast's eyeless draped over the top of his own like a hood. Nearly as massively built as Gaudfridus, he shrugged his burly shoulders and blinked pale blue eyes, startling in their red-skinned frame.

"Yes, as a matter of fact, we must. It is the only way to show respect to the animal I have slain. The wolf and I are one. I must respect the ways of the animal that lives within me."

The conviction in his response seemed to win over Jewel.

 "Why Berlot, do I spy more freckles on your face? They are so cute"

Stevyn fluttered his eyelashes and made a simpering sound that, combined with his sister's sweetly voiced mockery, drew splutters of laughter from their brethren. Weary of their bickering and complaints, Armin set his goblet down with a distinct clap of metal against bare stone. The sound drew his siblings' attention. When all directed their fearsome gazes toward him, he spoke:

 "Brothers, you know the rules. Section 213.7 of the Articles state that once a member has fallen, we must honor them by eating and drinking from the realm he or she protected. That is the law. There can be no order without the law. The great rebellion of the First Age taught us that. It is a tradition that has kept the Order strong for thousands of years, and it is that tradition we must honor and obey."

All heads bowed under the weight of his authority.

 "Now, let us feast."

Unseen but for flashes of white light, platters manifested before each of the Knights. Steam rose from the unappealing collection of foodstuffs, resulting in wrinkled noses and pressed lips. Amin the Divine scanned the table, ready to

pounce upon anyone who dared complain about the meal. Lucis looked especially queasy. The tone of his skin turned pale, and if one was to pay close attention, they would notice the slight spin of his head as his eyes rolled to the back of their sockets, and he fought to keep from hurling.

"This is heimel, the most popular meal in the whole of Thorton," he intoned. *"Enjoy."*

They ate in silence, but for the quiet clinking of cutlery and the sound of mastication. Anisau, blessed with super speed, gobbled everything down within seconds and belched in relief for having disposed of the awful meal. Jewel swallowed slowly and sipped from the goblet to wash the bland food down. Rising to his massive paws, Rupin's furred head appeared above the tabletop. The great beast sniffed at the plate. Its lips peeled back to reveal fearsome teeth, and a low growl rumbled up from its thick throat. The big cat chuffed, then turned away in disgust.

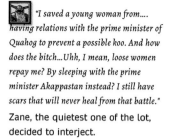

"Damn, even Rupin won't touch this stuff. I feel sorry for the people of Thorton," Stevyn murmured to Gaudfridus, who couldn't quite quell the snort that escaped.

The angel responded curtly as if offended by the comment

"You feel sorry for humans? You can't be serious?"

Jewel threw her hands up in the air in anticipation of the debate that was certain to arise from Stevyn's careless remark. Her eyes rolled twice, a foreshadowing response to what she expected to happen.

"Why? Why did you have to say THAT, Stevyn? You know how preachy Galdy gets, especially when he has a few spirits in him"

Gaudfridus paid her no mind and continued.

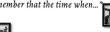

"I mean humans are so spoiled. I remember that the time when..."

"That's it. I'm out."

Jewel stood up hands over her ears trying desperately to escape the coming politics, a penetrating stare from Armin quickly changed her mind as plopped back down in her seat determined not to listen. Gaudfridus took advantage of the distraction, took another swig of his Derkji, which was clearly spiked with one of his tonics based on the glaze in his eyes, and continued.

"As I was saying, I remember the time I saved a young woman from the lust demon Srekkliah to prevent her from fucking..."

Armin interrupted. *"Watch the foul language, Gaudfridus! I know we are not bound by the same laws, but we can still have some manners at the table."*

Gaudfridus gave a slight nod in compliance.

"Like I was saying," he continued with the humility of a well-mannered child.

"I saved a young woman from.... having relations with the prime minister of Quahog to prevent a possible koo. And how does the bitch...Uhh, I mean, loose women repay me? By sleeping with the prime minister Akappastan instead? I still have scars that will never heal from that battle."

Zane, the quietest one of the lot, decided to interject.

"Galdy, I hear you, but have we not all suffered the same pain? What does it benefit us to relive these experiences over and over? Best not to let the past fester, with the dawn brings a new day!"

Azrael chimed in.

"Spoken like a true pacifist. No wonder you've never killed a demon."

Zane replied. *"Why kill when you can negotiate? My realm exists in perfect balance; good and evil working together."*

"Yeah... until the demons come to slit your throat in the middle of the night."

"What would give them a reason to do such a thing? We trade souls evenly; everyone gets their fair share."

"Simple my feeble-minded friend. It is a trap to lure you to sleep. All the while, a dagger hovers above you, ready to fall."

"Sound like paranoia to me, friend. Since when did the mind of Everlasting become so cynical?"

"Moves and Counter moves, brother. That is what I see."

Gaudfridus took back control of the conversation,

"Demons, I can understand. They want what we want. But these humans, these men, they base everything off feeling and emotion. Everything is fleeting, even their lifespan. So wishy-washy. Good one day, bad the next. I don't get them"

Raj decided to join in the rousing discussion.

 "It is a mystery, my friend dear. As the oldest of you, I once spent a whole millennium meditating on the subject. When I awoke, I reached enlightenment."

Gaudfridus sat tall in his chair, anxiously awaiting his reply,

"What was your revelation? Spit it out already!"

 "I awoke to the discovery that I knew nothing. To know nothing sometimes is more rewarding than to know all."

Gaudfridus leaned back, head hung in dismay,

"That's what you learned... Good Lord, you could have saved your breath on that one, Raj."

Lucis, laughing, could no longer hold his tongue,

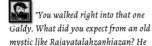 "You walked right into that one Galdy. What did you expect from an old mystic like Rajavatalahzanhiazan? He

will NEVER give you a straight answer."

Raj gave a small nod in agreement to Lucis's insightful remark.

Gaudfridus nodded as well, determined to make his point,

 "You all know what I am trying to say, humans get a pass. They can walk in the light and dark with no consequence. All because the Everlasting's Son decides..."

Jewel had been silent long enough. She knew just how to shut down this rhetoric for good before it got out of hand. She tapped her goblet with her fork, the noise drawing attention.

"Brothers, we should all toast to the honor of Artemus."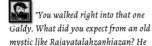

Her brethren nodded in approval and raised their glasses.

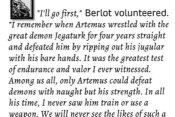 "I'll go first," Berlot volunteered. "I remember when Artemus wrestled with the great demon Jegaturk for four years straight and defeated him by ripping out his jugular with his bare hands. It was the greatest test of endurance and valor I ever witnessed. Among us all, only Artemus could defeat demons with naught but his strength. In all his time, I never saw him train or use a weapon. We will never see the likes of such a warrior again!"

"Here, here!" the family cheered.

 "I can do better. Brothers, do you remember when he took down those demon-possessed herd of gigabulls by himself?"

"Aye! Well spoke,"

His gold skin gleamed. He took a mouthful of the awful meal and choked it down before continuing to speak. "He prevented many from being impaled by their poisonous horns. "A plot concocted by the demon Traadus; I have no doubt. "

"The Protector!" the siblings shouted in chorus.

 "I got one. Remember when Artemus took on three shape-shifting demon witches from Argabith and returned with not a scratch on em'. Such strength and cunning are legendary!"

"The Protector! The Protector!" came the resounding chorus.

Azrael stood up,

 "The Dragon of Eastermont, twenty-feet tall with a forty-foot wingspan, scales as hard as iron and talon as sharp as razor-blades. The only beast that could breathe fire and ice at the same time. Legions of men dedicated their life to slaying the beast that plagued their people and destroyed their cities. Artemus took the beasts to head within a fortnight."

The Spectacular Feats of Artemus the Protector, Strength of the Everlasting

Years of Service : 1,037 years

# of Demons Slain : 10,357

Battles of Note:
- Killed 2,345 stampeding gigabulls with one blow
- Slayed the Dragon of Eastermont
- Eradicated the coven of witches from Argabith
- Defeated the Jegaturk the Giant

Weapon of Choice : Bare Hands

Favorite Move: Soul Breaker

Favorite Food : Heimel

Favorite Phrase: Weapons are for weaklings

Overcome with emotion, Reimund bellowed,

"Yes! Yes! Artemus the mighty! There will never be another like him. Let us vote now for his passage into the First Realm. He deserves to live forever."

Goblets clanged, and fists pounded the tabletop as the siblings shouted praises to honor their fallen brother and close friend. The reverberations of their chorus of voices stirred the heavens, inciting angels from all realms to join in the glorious choir of laud for the worthy warrior. White light glowed above them in the multicolored sky, a small spot that grew in size and reaches. The warriors joined hands and raised them high, their voices harmonizing to render an unbearably beautiful song of praise to their creator in memory of the fallen. The white light brightened, so intense that they all closed their eyes lest they are stricken blind.

When the light faded, the siblings lowered their hands and released their clasp. They opened their eyes, the platters and goblets vanished, leaving nothing but bare stone. It was done. The memorial had finished. Armin regretted what must come next, but their tradition mandated their subsequent actions.

"Knights of the Trinity," he began, commanding their attention with his quiet, solemn tone. *"It is now time to pass a vote for Artemus' safe passage to the First Realm and everlasting life. We must not shirk this duty, no matter how difficult, this charge given to us by Archangel Michael."*

Heads all around bowed beneath the weight of their holy obligation. Armin continued, stalwart as always.

"As you know, brothers, only one of us—the greatest of the Knights—will be permitted into the First Realm of heaven and enjoy everlasting life, free from death to live out eternity in peace. I know it is tempting to think of ourselves when it comes to the vote, but we are charged with the responsibility to be selfless in the selection process, a process I know we all take seriously like you have done many times before."

All heads nodded in compliance.

"Without further ado, let us begin. All those in favor of Artemus receiving safe passage into the First Realm? Raise your hand and say 'aye' when I call your name."

Armin called out each sibling's name, including his own. Each of the brethren gave his response, resulting in a split vote of eight in favor and four against.

Here we go again, he thought and rolled his eyes, hoping that none of his contentious siblings noticed. The last memorial ceremony two centuries ago resulted in the same lack of consensus. However, tradition obligated him to proceed through the process, which had yet to yield a consensus vote advancing one of their kind into the First Realm.

"Since we do not have consensus, let the debate for Artemus begin," he announced.

Two days passed without consensus. Gaudfridus and Stevyn convinced Lucis to change his vote to approve their fallen brother's passage. Raj and Armin swung the opinions of Berlot and Jewel to vote against them. With a deadlock of six against six, the third day promised nothing but heartache.

Armin remembered the last vote vexed the relationship between Lucis and Zane so much that they avoided speaking to one another for three hundred thirty-seven years. Reluctant to witness such enmity between siblings again, he decided to put an end to their increasingly hostile bickering.

He pounded his fist on the table, causing the others to jolt upright in their seats. The surprise at their brother's sudden display of intense passion, which was uncharacteristic of his nature, had startled them and commanded their full attention.

"Brothers, Knights, Angels! Enough squabbling. We are better than this. This is the seven hundred fifty-sixth selection process that I have had the distinguished honor to host, and it would be remiss if it ends—yet again—in brothers feuding against each other."

They looked at him, eyes filled with glowing admiration, while a numbered few among them, took enmity at his words. The friction of disdain crowding the space between them, some with more animosity than others. Armin, the Divine continued.

 "We are each gifted with the sight, the ability to see a being's history, his good, and bad deeds. Artemus was a great angel, a valiant knight of the Trinity, and an eradicator of evil. No one debates that. However, we all know he struggled with his love of leaf and ale while assigned to Thorton."

He paused to let the words sink in.

 "Is that the kind of Knight we want to represent us in the First Realm, the closest to the Everlasting?"

The angels held their silence as they contemplated Armin's argument. All agreed they needed a good night's rest before casting their final vote on the third day. Armin gladly dismissed them, if only to bring a temporary cease-fire to their squabbling.

The night passed quickly, too brief a reprieve from arguments and flares of temper. Armin rejoined his brethren, once again wearing the elaborate ceremonial robes that pulled at his shoulders as though made from sanding paper, ripping away at the outer layer of his skin as if refining it with a pumice stone. Although, from the outside looking in, it glowed in all the treasures of the purest gold.

He looked around to those gathered at the table. Giving time to gaze into the faces of each of his brothers and sisters. They eagerly waited to finalize the casting of their individual ballots so the matter would once and for all be behind them.

The Tournament of Heroes stole the bulk of their interest, and soon their votes were completed. White light blinked, and full goblets of the fizzy blue Thorton ale appeared in front of each of them.

Armin, the Divine, took a deep breath and calmed his spirit.

 "Are we ready? All those in favor of"

"Don't I get a vote?"

bellowed a voice from a distance. Perturbed by the interruption of this vitally important business, Armin slowly turned to see who spoke. He glowered in recognition, his heart pounded, and his breath became shallow and rapid.

none of the speed it manifested. Silver armor embossed with intricate markings encased the herculean figure, dwarfing the siblings with the sheer immensity of height and breadth. The diamond handle of his massive war hammer protruded above the top of his helm, sparkling in the golden light and reflecting the rainbow sky. A malicious smile spread across Lucis's face. He leaned toward Gaudfridus and whispered,

 "This is going to be good. These two hate each other. Let's watch Armin's skin crawl."

Gaudfridus snickered.

Armin rolled his eyes again, not caring whether his siblings saw it.

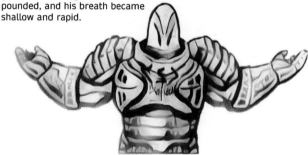

The speaker approached with a slow, deliberate stride that conveyed

 "Absolution, I did not know you would be here," Armin greeted their guest. "What are you doing here?"

"Don't worry, Armin, I'm not going to ruin your little party. No need to be scared."

Armin stiffened in righteous indignation at the taunt, but he held his silence.

"If anything, I came to liven things up."

The helm turned to face each of those gathered around the table None of the Order knew what complexion lay beneath the armor, given to Absolution by Archangel Michael himself. He continued,

"Gotta loosen up that fancy silk dress you're wearing and have some fun, for God's sake!"

HA HA HA HA HA HA !

Laughter erupted from Stevyn, Gaudfridus, and Jewel, both spewing Thorton ale from their mouths and their noses. The rest of the Knights were not so amused. They stared blankly, devoid of the jovial nature from their comrades.

Do they think I want to wear this fancy get-up? Now he has them laughing at me. I must nip this in the bud or lose their respect.

Armin did not voice his angry thoughts but gasped in disgust.

 "You know, taking the Lord's name in vain like that is against our credo! Don't you know the penalty for such blasphemy?"

"Yes, I do. The problem here is that none of you has the guts to carry it out."

The expressionless helm focused on Armin.

"Would you like to try, little man? I'll let you change out of your skirt and don proper armor first."

HA HA HA HA HA HA !

More laughter erupted, and Armin fumed, barely resisting the urge to tear the overly elaborate robes from his body.

.

"Anointed ones, why argue on such a fine day?"

The bell-like tones of Archangel Michael rang through the air. The laughter subsided, overwhelmed by the forceful presence of its bearer.

 "Absolution stand down. Armin, continue with your vote. I wish to see how this turns out."

Subdued by the nearly blinding magnificence of the archangel who wielded the Sword of God, the siblings whispered among themselves. Minutes of heated, albeit quiet, debate passed before they reached consensus.

Armin approached the archangel, head bowed, and said,

 "We Knights of the Trinity believe Artemus a true warrior worthy of the highest distinction and honor. However, we cannot agree to grant him passage to the First Realm and the reward of eternal life and

bliss. He will be enshrined in the Catacombs of Heroes, and he will receive a full page in the Golden Book of Knights."

A snort came from inside Absolution's silvery helm.

"Well, what a surprise--another fallen warrior not worthy of eternal life. This is such folly. Armin knows this lot would never vote anyone in, except for themselves."

Usually, the most easygoing of the brothers, Raj took offense.

 "Are you questioning my honor, sir?"

"No," Absolution replied, his harsh voice ringing with truth.

"I know all of you are honorable. However, your ambition and narcissism are legendary. I don't know why you want to hang out with those shitbags anyway. The realms of man are weak and pathetic."

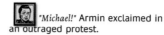 *"Michael!"* Armin exclaimed in an outraged protest.

"How long must we endure this outsider? You know scouts are not permitted on these sacred grounds, yet you allow him to sully it, to mock us and question our honor? I demand that you remove him."

Archangel Michael replied in an icy tone that wielded a blade sharper than Jewel's and holding the immense power of divine authority,

"No... and the next time you question me, it will be your passage to the First Realm of heaven under debate."

A light breeze ruffled the angel's golden curls as each of the mighty siblings met his gaze and submitted to his will, his word, and his authority. In a softer tone, he said,

"Now that we have mourned another fallen soldier and the ugly business of ascension is concluded, let's get on with the selection process."

Armin bowed his hand and clasped his hands. He took a deep breath, then looked up and met the cowed gazes of each of his siblings.

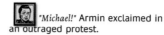 *"Brothers, as much as we loved Artemus, a new warrior must be chosen to replace him for tradition dictates that we must always have twelve. Twelve divine warriors committed to divine service. Who among you knows a worthy replacement?"*

THE WARRIOR BRETHREN TOSSED THE NAMES OF THE SCOUTS THEY FELT DESERVED TO SIT AMONG THEIR RANKS; YOUNG RECRUITS EXPERTLY TRAINED BY EACH WARRIOR FOR THE CHANCE TO BECOME ONE OF THE EVERLASTING'S ANOINTED SOLDIERS. ONLY THOSE WHO EXHIBITED EXTREME PROWESS, CUNNING, AND STAMINA WOULD BE CHOSEN. THEY SMILED AMONG THEMSELVES, ANTICIPATING THE TOURNAMENT OF HEROES AND THE THRILL OF COMBAT.

SOME THINGS JUST NEVER GOT OLD, EVEN FOR IMMORTALS.

2 | Right of Passage

EPISODE TWO
Out of eight hopefuls, a new Knight of the
Everlasting Order is crowned.

"BEHOLD, OUR NEWEST MEMBER OF THE EVERLASTING ORDER" – Armin

Resonant voices reverberated through the Third Realm. "Knights, let your selections come forward and enter the tournament!"

Each Knight turned to face the vast area between their table and the golden gates. The Knights turned, observing the scope of the divide between their place and the golden gates. The breath of air caressed their shoulders and glistened as brilliant as crystals.

THE ATMOSPHERE SHIMMERED, AND THE CLOUDS UPON WHICH THEY WALKED COALESCED INTO FINE SAND WHITE GLITTERING LIKE SNOW. A STRUCTURE OF AN ANCIENT GLORY MATERIALIZED AROUND THE CIRCLE OF SAND; however, instead of bleacher seating, it had one kingly chair for each of the cavaliers. The thirteenth seat drew ocular attention with its gold appointments and purple drapery.

Michael sat upon this particular seat, shifting just a little to make sure he didn't muss his snowy wings or bend a pristine feather. One by one, the Knights took their seats and called out the names of their champions. As each did so, the massive doors beneath opened, and their scouts entered the arena.

The seraphs practically glowed with anticipation. They had trained for this moment, this tourney, which would determine which of them would take a coveted seat as one of the Everlasting's chosen Knights. Their battle gear shined beneath the flaxen glow of divinity as they brandished a fearsome array of weapons blessed by the divine power himself.

 "Assemble before me young hopefuls"

EIGHT WOULD-BE CHAMPIONS OBEYED AND WAITED WHILE THE ARCHANGEL DREW LOTS TO DETERMINE WHICH OF THE SCOUTS WOULD SPAR FIRST.

Disciplined by their masters, they showed no outward sign of anxiety, although none had fought in such a glorified arena nor for such honor. Michael's piercing eyes saw through their bravado into their souls: he knew their fear of failure, their lack of assurance. It reminded him of the stirring in his belly when he first pledged his sword to the Order. The thought had the edges of his lips turn upward. He was well pleased with how far he had come.

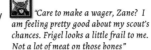 *"In the first round, Frigel and Kedtriel will battle!"*

Zane and Jewel's champions marched to the center of the arena, equally matched in fearsome appearance. They bowed to Michael, then to one another, a gesture of respect, yet a sure assurance of battle readiness.

 "Care to make a wager, Zane? I am feeling pretty good about my scout's chances. Frigel looks a little frail to me. Not a lot of meat on those bones"

"Does he now? I can assure you that he has been trained well. I would have it no other way."

 "Put your money where your mouth is then. I wager ten demons that my Kedtriel will win within the one day of conflict, an easy win for sure."

"Aww, you know me well, sweet sister. I can never say no for a chance at the good stuff. Well played, I accept your terms."

 Michael snapped his fingers. An inconspicuous cherub blew his horn in the distance; the tournament had begun.

JEWELL'S CHAMPION, KEDTRIEL, CHARGED FORWARD LIKE A BEAST, NEWLY RELEASED, AND READY FOR THE KILL. FRIGEL SIDESTEPPED THE BOLD ATTACK AND, WITH A SWIFT BLOW, IMPALED HIS ADVERSARY WITH A STRIKE TO THE PELVIS. KEDTRIEL STAMMERED BACK A FEW PACES BEFORE REGAINING HIS BALANCE. HIS STRIDE HAD BEEN INTERRUPTED FOR JUST A BRIEF MOMENT, BUT HE QUICKLY RECOVERED. A HARRIED SWIPE WITH HIS MUSCULAR LEG SENT HIS OPPONENT CRASHING TO THE GROUND, AND AT FRIGEL'S FEET. TAKING FULL ADVANTAGE OF THE BLUNDER, FRIGEL PLUNGED THE POINT OF HIS SHARPENED SPEAR INTO KEDTRIEL'S OPPONENT'S CHEST AND WATCHED AS DEATH'S THROES CAUSED HIS BODY TO CONVULSE IN EPILEPTIC VIBRATIONS. SWEAT SHOWERED THE CROWN OF HIS HEAD AS HE FOUGHT HIS MORBID DESTINY WITH MORE SKILL THAN HE DISPLAYED IN THE ACTUAL BATTLE. THE AIR IN HIS LUNGS, RELEASING ITSELF INTO OBLIVION AS KEDTRIEL TOOK HIS LAST BREATH, WAS THE SIGN OF FRIGEL'S VICTORY. IT WAS ONLY WHEN THE BODY WENT LIMP, DID THE VICTOR WITHDREW THE TIP OF THE BLADE FROM HIS OPPONENT'S HEART.

FRIGEL YANKED OUT HIS SPEAR AND SET IT BUTT END DOWN IN THE SAND, HEEDLESS OF THE BLOOD THAT TRICKLED DOWN THE BLADE AND SHAFT. He waited in respectful silence until Michael nodded to acknowledge his victory while Jewell muttered under her breath about the utter incompetence of the scout, she'd trained herself:

 'Idiot. Fool. Clumsy ass."

She glared at Zane's elation etched into the creases of his forehead. His face, adorned in confidence, veiled the joy he felt as a result of her scowl. He knew the embarrassment that came with such a quick defeat, and regardless he dared not to get on Jewel's bad side. Seeing that Zane was not going to give her the satisfaction she desired, she focused her attention on his scout.

Her lip curled in a sneer.

 "If I didn't know any better, I'd swear you cheated. You'll regret that"

she threatened and glared at Frigel, who turned pale with fright and looked to his master for support.

Zane gave no comfort or reassurance. Frigel's fate was now in the hands of a brother of the Everlasting. As much as he objected to her allegations, Zane nor any other knight would ever take the side of a scout over the bonds of brotherhood; the young warrior was on his own. Frigel bowed his head and kneeled in front of Jewel, kissing her feet as a sign of respect.

"Do you accept my victory? If not, I will gladly give my life in payment for offending you"

"You trained him how to grovel, that is for sure"

Her comment was made to her counterpart but said boisterously enough to be intentionally heard by all.

"I accept your victory but stay out of my sight for the rest of the tournament. You can GO now"

She dismissed him with a quick wave of her hand.

Zane gave a nod of thanks to Jewel for sparing Frigel's life. He made no mention of collecting the debt owed. Better to wait until the tournament was over and cooler heads prevailed.

Michael gave pause until the sniping ceased, then he looked at Armin, who sat to his immediate right and muttered privately,

"That was fast. I came to see warriors battle, not hand maiden's mud wrestle. Are you sure this lot is properly trained? "At this rate, the tournament will be over before I finish my drink."

Armin pinched the bridge of his nose and sighed.

Michael drew lots for the second round, which pitched Gaudfridus' champion, Tagerk, against Lucis' champion, Snertum.

AT THE ARCHANGEL'S DESULTORY NOD, THE TWO WARRIOR ANGELS CHARGED AT EACH OTHER. THE HISS AND CLANG OF SWORDS FILLED THE ARENA, UNDERSCORED BY GRUNTS OF EFFORT AND THE RASP OF SAND. THE KNIGHTS, EXCEPT FOR JEWEL, WATCHED RAPT AS SNERTUM PUT TAGERK ON THE DEFENSE, THE LATTER RETREATING. WHEN SNERTUM POISED TO STRIKE, ONE GAUNTLETED HAND GRIPPING HIS OPPONENT'S FOREARM, TAGERK TWISTED FREE. THE KNIGHTS WATCHED IN ADMIRATION AS TAGERK RECOILED AND LUNGED, THRUSTING HIS SWORD INTO SNERTUM'S BELLY. THE PALE ARMOR YIELDED TO THE HOLY BLADE,

OFFERING NO RESISTANCE. AS THE ANGEL BENT OVER THE RAZOR-SHARP EDGE IMPALING HIM, TAGERK DREW THE BATTLE-AX SLUNG BETWEEN HIS SHOULDERS AND SWUNG. SNERTUM'S HEAD FLEW ACROSS THE ARENA, BOUNCED, AND ROLLED TO A HALT BENEATH HIS MASTER'S SEAT. INSIDE HIS EYES WAS A SADNESS, HIS LAST EXPRESSION BEFORE DEATH TOOK HIM.

"Yes! Yes! I told you that boy had no business quarreling with a real man! I may be old, but I still have cranked out more champions than the lot of you."

Lucis shook his head in silent acceptance of his champion's defeat.

"Good victory, old man. Not my best showing, I will admit, There is always next time."

"Next time, Ha! The familiar words of a loser."

Lucis just smiled and nodded. There was no use arguing with the old goat.

Assuming a bored mien, Michael drew the next two lots: Dire representing Armin and Rewmer representing Berlot.

into the arena and prowled along the marble wall. Rupin directed his predatory gaze at Yeddai and growled every time Clandor delivered a blow.

Rupin dragged Yeddai's carcass aside with his massive paws, intent to make a meal of him.

 "That's cheating!"

 "Says who?"

 "Cease"

Armin shouted before the two Knights could even begin to clash. He jumped down, driving himself between the two warriors.

This round took longer than the first yet not as long as the second, ending with Dire's tall and slender build looming over Rewmer's lifeless form, his sword lodged between the defeated angel's eyes.

In the fourth round, Reimund's Yeddai fought against Stevyn's Clandor. Stevyn's beast leaped

The sabertooth cat's ominous, threatening presence unnerved Yeddai, which gave Clandor advantage. That slight edge was all the warrior needed to carry out the crushing blow to Yeddai's skull and obtain a hard-fought victory.

"Your big dumb cat distracted Yeddai, and now you add to the disrespect by EATING him? I will KILL you for the dishonor!"

Reimund drew his bow and jumped into the arena. Stevyn drew his field knife and prepared himself for battle.

The other two fighters towered over him, yet neither dared engage him in battle--at least not separately. Though slender and insubstantial next to most of them, none of them had ever defeated him when sparring.

Their leader's prowess, seldom displayed against them, also commanded their respect.

 "He clearly cheated, Armin. My champion would have won if that mangy beast would not have interfered. I want Clandor beheaded for the offense. An eye for an eye is the only way to settle this"

"A true champion worthy of the Order would not allow the nuisance of kitty-cat's caterwauling to distract him in battle. I suggest you end this protest and take your seat."

Armin cowed him with an icy glare.

Reimund opened his mouth to retort but decided that holding his tongue would be the better option.

Rupin, bloodthirsty from his fresh meal, gave into animal instinct and tried to maul Armin from behind. Armin lashed out violently at the cat as it leaped toward him. The feline beast

yowled from the strike, hit the ground and rolled, and raced back to his master for consoling. Stevyn dared smile. Armin rounded on him, his upper lip curling into a sneer.

 "You either control that ill-mannered cat, or I will."

Stevyn's smile disappeared. He nodded, turned on his heel, commanded Rupin to leave the fallen Yeddai in peace, and went back to his seat.

Berlot commented in a futile attempt to mollify Reimund.

 "On the bright side Rey, at least your champion lasted longer than Jewel's"

they all were waiting for someone to make the jest. Even Michael got a rise from Berlot's impeccable comedic timing.

You know, it's days like this when I really hate you guys"

Jewell griped, beet red and arms folded. Her warrior's defeat loomed large in her thoughts, stinging her pride. She knew it might be another millennium before her cohorts stopped telling the tale of Kedtriel, the charging buffoon.

 "Enough"

Michael commanded unbothered by the antics, or the amusing undertones. Glowering, the Knights obeyed. Michael drew lots again, pitting champions of the first round of matches against each other.

ENTERING THE ARENA AND IGNORING THE CARCASSES OF THE DEFEATED CHAMPIONS, TAGERK FACED DIRE. WITH RENEWED FEROCITY, THEY CHARGED TOWARD ONE ANOTHER. DIRE PUMMELED TAGERK'S CHEST WITH A BARRAGE OF CALCULATED SWORD ATTACKS, DELIVERING AN UNYIELDING RUSH OF BRUTE FORCE. REELING BACKWARD, TAGERK ABSORBED THE SHOCK AND DROVE HIS FIST INTO DIRE'S RIBS. THE ATTACK FOLLOWED COUNTERATTACK, WEAPONS CLASHED, AND MASSIVE TAGERK LAUNCHED HIMSELF INTO A SOMERSAULT THAT TOOK DIRE BY SURPRISE. HE JABBED A DAGGER INTO DIRE'S THIGH. DIRE'S WOUNDED LEG BUCKLED, AND TAGERK MOVED IN FOR THE KILL. BUT DIRE HAD ONE LAST TRICK THAT LEFT TAGERK STARING AT THE JEWELED HILT OF A SWORD PROTRUDING FROM HIS HEART. A SECOND LATER, THE LIGHT OF AWARENESS WENT OUT OF HIS EYES. DIRE HAD CLAIMED THE VICTORY.

"Hey, Galdy, you old goat, I don't hear you boasting now!"

Gaudfridus took the high road and tipped his helm to Armin for a job well done.

"You trained him well, Armin, no shame in losing to someone with such skill."

Armin nodded back in a show of respect.

FRIGEL STEPPED INTO THE RING, KICKING TAGERK'S BODY ASIDE. CLANDOR FACED HIM AND FLEXED HIS MUSCLES BENEATH HIS ARMOR. IT WAS AN UNSEEN NARCISSISTIC REMINDER TO HIMSELF THAT HE WAS WELL CAPABLE OF BEING THE CHAMPION. AFTER A MOMENT OF TENSE SILENCE AND MEASURING, THE RIVALS CRASHED TOGETHER IN A RINGING CLOUD OF BLOODY VIOLENCE THAT ECHOED WITH FRIGEL'S DYING SCREAM, THE EXTRACTION OF BLOOD SPILLING FROM HIS BODY, MAKING SEPARATE POOLS OF SCARLET TO COLOR THE GROUND BENEATH HIM.

It was down to the final two warriors. Michael allowed the scouts a brief respite but did not order the removal of the bodies of the defeated. It was down to the final two warriors. Michael allowed the scouts a brief respite but did not order the removal of the bodies of the defeated. The obstacles littering the arena and the prowling sabertooth cat made things a little more challenging and, therefore, more enjoyable in his mind.

Finally, Dire and Clandor took their places near the center of the ring. Dire hefted his four sabers, blades glinting beneath the golden light of his armor.

His slim build, including four scrawny arms, looked insubstantial next to his prominent, burly opponent.

Clandor's brassy armor resembled his master's with sharp spikes and jagged edges designed to pierce and shred.

Clandor raised his gauntleted fists, preferring to defeat his rivals with the brute force of his bare hands rather than edged weapons. The horn blew as the brotherhood stomped the ground beneath them. The final battle had begun.

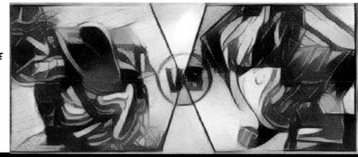

THE TWO WARRIOR ANGELS CLASHED, TRADING BLOW FOR BLOW.

FROM THEIR SEATS, THE KNIGHTS LEANED FORWARD IN ANTICIPATION, SHOUTING ENCOURAGEMENT TO THEIR FAVORITE. ARMIN HUNG HID HEAD AND MUTTERED OBSCENITIES UNDER HIS BREATH, KNOWING THE OUTCOME BEFORE HIS CHAMPION DID. USING NOTHING MORE THAN THE BRUTE FORCE OF HIS FISTS AND MIGHT, CLANDOR CRUSHED HIS WORTHY OPPONENT. FIRST, HE SKILLFULLY SHATTERED TWO OF DIRE'S BLADES USING JAGGED ARMOR. DESPERATE TO RETALIATE, DIRE HASTILY THRUST THE REMAINING TWO SWORDS INTO CLANDOR'S GUT. IT WAS NOTHING MORE THAN AN INCONVENIENT TICKLE TO HIM THANKS TO HIS THICK ARMOR AND HERCULEAN FRAME. ARMIN HAD ADVISED HIM OF THE WEAK SPOTS IN CLANDOR'S ARMOR, BUT DIRE'S WITS LEFT HIM IN THE CHAOS OF BATTLE. CLANDOR TOOK FULL ADVANTAGE; HE THEN WRAPPED HIS ARMS AROUND DIRE, FLIPPED HIM UPSIDE DOWN, AND JUMPED,

DRIVING DIRE'S HELMETED HEAD INTO THE GROUND. THE CRACK OF DIRE'S NECK REVERBERATED THROUGHOUT THE REALM, FOLLOWED BY THE RASP HEAVING BREATH AND THE RATTLE OF DIRE'S DEATH THROES.

The Seventh Spark – Knights of the Trinity

From his seat, Armin boomed,

"Behold! From the house of Stevyn, our new member of the Everlasting Order, a Knights of the Trinity!"

His voice revealed none of the dismay or disappointment he may have felt now that his apprentice Dire lay lifeless, face buried in the Oracle sands.

Armin raised his hands

"Congratulations, Knight. Our fallen brother, Artemus, now passes his gift on to you."

"Behold, Clandor the Mighty, you are the strength of the Everlasting!"

As the echo of his words reverberated throughout the realm, a blinding light filled the arena. Clandor raised his arms, the heavy plates of his armor crinkling like paper and falling back to reveal dense, bulging muscle. Divine lightning crackled overhead and struck, congealing in a new manifestation of his predecessor's armor, shiny and unmarred by the rigor and damage of combat. The influx of power made his great body convulse. Clandor dropped to his knees, unable to remain standing beneath the onslaught of power that now coursed through his body. His teeth chattered, though he felt neither cold nor hot. His hands clenched into mighty fists. His head bowed in submission to the divinity that filled him with its formidable strength. Heaving great breaths, Clandor looked at his fists. They glowed. His gaze traveled over his own body, and he gaped at the light emanating from it. He threw his head back and opened and closed his fists, feeling the power piercing through him.

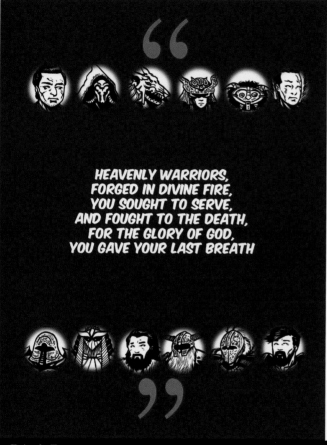

> HEAVENLY WARRIORS,
> FORGED IN DIVINE FIRE,
> YOU SOUGHT TO SERVE,
> AND FOUGHT TO THE DEATH,
> FOR THE GLORY OF GOD,
> YOU GAVE YOUR LAST BREATH

It was almost too much for him to handle. He decided to test himself. With a great bound, he leaped into the center of the arena and pounded his fist into the dirt. White sand exploded in a grainy fountain as a shockwave of power rumbled through the earth, a violent shaking that shook the Knights off their feet. Even the Archangel found himself unsettled, spilling his wine. The purplish liquid splattered the smooth skin of his chest, the pristine white of his clothes, and the luxurious velvet draped over the stone.

Reveling in the awesome power granted him, Clandor stood and smiled at the unmarred gauntlet, apparently as firm and durable as he felt. The other Knights righted themselves and alternated between glaring at their newest member and darting fretful glances at the Archangel. They sighed in audible relief when Michael sat upright and raised his glass. Laughing with unexpected merriment, he cried out,

 "That is the best thing I have seen all day. Well done, Clandor! My new Knight of the Everlasting Order, may you serve well."

The Knights stood and cheered, welcoming their newest member to leave the arena and join them at the table. The chair formerly occupied by Artemus creaked beneath Clandor's substantial weight. Seated, they all hoisted goblets in a silent toast to the victor.

Once they quaffed their thirst, Armin rose to his feet once more and said,

"Now, let us honor the dead"

The other Knights rose and sang as hosts of lesser angels carried the bodies from the Oracle. As the last note died away, the dry sand dissolved into a cloud, and the marble walls faded into nothingness. No sign remained of the fallen, except for the somber mood of those who remained.

The single clap of Armin's hand resounded like the crack of lightning, capturing everyone's attention. He intoned,

 "Anointed ones, it is time to celebrate our newest addition, Clandor! Feast my brethren, be merry"

He clapped his hands again. Light flashed over the table, leaving behind a sumptuous feast of the Knights' favorite cuisines and jugs of wine. Rousing music of victory filled the air. Gaudfridus, once mournful, grabbed the charred leg of fowl and took a huge bite, followed by a big gulp of the

good stuff he had been hoarding to himself. Armin filled his plate and goblet and carried them away from the table to dine in peaceful solitude. Stevyn grabbed a pig's haunch and tossed it over his shoulder. Rupin leaped and caught the offering in mid-air. Zane finally worked up the nerve to ask Jewel to make good on their bet. She reluctantly complied, cursing under her breath as she took some jars out her satchel. These were not ordinary jars; the glasses were marked with ancient symbols, spells to contain, or perhaps change the remains confined inside. Zane was giddy with excitement as he opened one and took a whiff.

 "This is a rather weak one, such a pity, not much essence at all, not in a generous mood I see."

Jewel responded curtly,

"The bet was for ten demons, you failed to negotiate strength these demons need be to qualify. A deal is a deal."

"Well said. I think I will have one now and leave the rest for later."

"Fine by me, but if Armin catches you with those..."

"I know, I know, I will not rat you out" The boy scout will never know. Now, let me enjoy my sweet reward in peace."

Jewel left Zane to himself. It was not wise to be around another angel while they partook in such activities. Consuming the essence of a demon was a dangerous thing, not forbidden, but heavily frowned upon by all accounts. It was reserved for the mightiest of Angels. Few could handle the hallucinogenic effects, but even fewer could contain the immense power it gave the consumer.

ZANE INHALED DEEPLY, SMOKE FILLING HIS LUNGS. HE HELD HIS BREATH AND CLOSED HIS LIPS TIGHTLY. IT WOULD BE A PITY TO WASTE ANY OF THE

REMAINS. ALL HE HAD TO DO NOW WAS WAIT. TEN SECONDS OR SO SHOULD DO THE TRICK. HE STARTED COUNTING BACKWARD IN HIS HEAD. 10, 9, 8... THE SENSATION ROLLED OVER HIM LIKE THE TIDE. THE RUSH OF EXCITEMENT, LUST, POWER, DECEPTION, FEAR, PRIDE, CHAOS. A BUFFET OF SIN WITHOUT THE SIDE EFFECT OF GUILT OR SHAME, PURE CONCENTRATED EVIL. A SENSATION AN ANGEL COULD NEVER ACHIEVE ON THEIR OWN. IT DIDN'T LAST LONG. THE PURITY OF ZANE'S SPIRIT QUICKLY SUBDUED THE OUT OF BODY EXPERIENCE. LIKE ANTIBODIES KILLING A VIRUS, A FLEETING MOMENT OF ECSTASY FOLLOWED BY A RELAXING CALMNESS AS EVIL TURNED TO GOOD, DARKNESS TO LIGHT.

ZANE LET OUT A LONG BELCH, BREATHED DEEP, FILLING HIS LUNGS, AND WAITED FOR THE SECOND PHASE TO COME. HIS SPIRIT QUICKENED, HEART RACING IN ANTICIPATION. AND THEN IT HAPPENED, THE QUICKENING— A ROUSING BURST OF POWER.

ZANE'S HANDS TREMBLED; HIS EYES ROLLED INTO THE BACK OF HIS HEAD. HE COULD FEEL HIMSELF GETTING STRONGER, WISER, A BETTER VERSION OF HIS FORMER SELF. A TRANSFORMATION, THE REBIRTH OF ZANE. A BETTER ZANE THAN THE ONE BEFORE HIM.

As quickly as it started, it was over. The warrior closed his eyes and breathed slowly to cherish the moment. When he opened them, he promptly stashed the rest of his bounty into his satchel and rejoined his quarry. It was not wise to linger. On his way back, he noticed the Archangel, Michael, having a private conversation with Lucis. The two went off together, tied at the hip, in full throat. Were they reminiscing about old times, or perhaps prophesying about the future to come? He could not say; however, he knew better than to eavesdrop on Michael's conversations. What he did know is that when Michael summons

you, it is for something important. He was an angel of purpose and rarely engaged in idle conversations.

Absolution watched from the wings, unable to share the joy and celebration. He glanced into the blurry distance where the lesser angels in the second realm resided—the realm where he once lived, until Armin's invitation. Absolution never knew why he was spared. He feared to ask. He never stopped resenting his exclusion from the Knights' ranks. No matter how many demons fell beneath the power of his mighty Warhammer, the Knights always considered him a charity case, the Archangel's servant, a failure who should have died. He would never enter their ranks, for there were no repeats, no second chances.

He glanced at Armin, who dined alone and watched the celebration with a contemplative air. The wisest Knight must have felt his regard and turned his dark eyes to him.

Resentment and loneliness swelled within his heart. Just that once, he needed companionship, even if it were of the adversarial variety.

"Armin, care to continue our spar, brother? I am certain the outcome would be different this time."

"I am not your brother, errand boy. A scout can never be a brother to an anointed Knight. Have you forgotten?"

"Forgotten? How could I? You remind me every chance you get."

"Fact is, anointed or not; you will never have as many demon trophies as I. They don't call me Demon's Bane for nothing."

Armin blinked, unmoved by the response.

"Perhaps not, but at least my name will be entered in the Golden Book of Heroes, and maybe I will ascend to the First Heaven and be awarded eternal life. You will never have the chance, lowly scout"

Beneath his helm, Absolution flushed at the chastisement uttered in a dispassionate, crisp tone. No, he would never have that chance, and the reminder galled him.

"Perhaps. I have no desire to associate with those meatbags, anyway. The realms of men disgust me. I mean, why are men so special? What makes those cretins so great? Because the Everlasting had a son with one of their women?"

"Blasphemy! How have you escaped Lucifer's fate all this time is beyond me."

"That's easy. I will tell you a secret, brother. Our divine leader favors the bold. The Everlasting has no interest in your petty rules, doctrines, and procedures. He is interested in the brazen, the unheralded, the rebels. How else can explain my power without the blessing of the Everlasting?"

"Ridiculous. Our code--our rules--have stood since the beginning of time itself. You mock our forebears, our traditions. Do you hold anything sacred?"

Armin's icy glare held Absolution's defiant gaze while the latter gathered his thoughts,

 "Yes, I do, brother"

 "The annihilation of evil under the brute force of my Warhammer--that is my code. That is my standard!"

A small smile of what could have been approval curved the corners of Armin's mouth,

"Finally, we can agree on something. Let's have a drink."

Astounded by invitation, said without a tinge of contempt, Absolution's antagonism withered. He would not decline this unprecedented opportunity.

 "Now, you're talking. To Artemis!"

"To Artemis!"

They each took a long drink from their goblets. Choking, Armin spewed blue fizz, coating his silk robe.

 "This Derkji is terrible! To think I made you guys drink this sludge."

"Well, at least the blue splatter matches your fine silk dress. It is an improvement."

Absolution clapped him on the back and laughed. Armin smiled and laughed, too.

3 | The Invitation

"Armin often brags about your skill with a blade. Let's if the tales are true. - Michael

The distant sounds of celebration floated upon the pure, sparkling air of the Third Realm beckoned Lucis to rejoin his brethren, but he resisted. Sitting on the ground and leaning back against an ancient tree's mighty trunk, Lucis looked up as the golden sky dimmed to burnt orange and then to a velvety brown. Swirls of green, pink, and pale blue light flashed above, reminiscent of the aurora borealis in Eon's arctic or the colors embedded in fire opal.

Lucis held an honest affection for God's amazing palette of colors. He never tired of watching light dance upon the oceans or filter through a canopy of leaves. He loved the way dust danced golden and gleaming in beams of light or the sparkle of snow like crushed diamonds poured over the ground. He saw it as divine magic, an energy that was pure,

holy, and absent of evil.

Lucis felt the presence of another and glanced to see who had joined him. Michael eased down beside him, stretching out his long legs. The corner of his mouth quirked upward as the Archangel's golden curls waved gently as though a light breeze played with them. Lucis would never dare accuse Michael of vanity, but he thought his affectation was a little on the silly side. Perhaps his hair danced from a well-concealed sense of humor. That thought brought a smile to Lucis's face. He was quick to hide it.

Michael remained an enigma to the rest of the Order. He was a cut above, the highest of holy warriors, his place already elevated beyond what any mere Knight could ever achieve.

After all, he was the angel who defeated Lucifer himself and drove him out of heaven. The realms of men sang songs and even worshipped him, a feat Lucis could never hope to receive, especially as Lucifer's replacement.

 "Noisy little beasts, aren't they?"

Michael murmured in the round, mellifluous tones that would have made any orator swoon with envy.

 "The celebration is well deserved; I don't begrudge them the joy and pleasure of it."

"But you don't revel in it, either. Perhaps you're starting mature beyond a mere mindless brute."

 "Perhaps. I still get my kicks from watching old Galdy dance when he has too much to drink"

Michael smiled at that remark but continued to probe,

"Maybe you're starting to realize the

folly of it all. It's only a matter of time before we lose the next Knight and suffer the tedium of another tournament. I grow tired of futility of it."*

"Yes," Lucis replied carefully. He could see Michael was in a mood, now was not the time for debate.

"I see your point"

They sat in companionable quiet-- or as sociable as one might get in proximity to the mighty Archangel--until Lucis shifted position.

"You're restless. Perhaps you're spending too much time in choir rehearsal, rather than actual training,"

"Perhaps ... It is not easy juggling both. The other Knights only have to concern themselves with man's bickering. I get both man and angels; at times we can be worse"

Michael smirked and rose to his feet with smooth, fluid strength unencumbered by the bulk and weight of armor and weaponry. Lucis tried to remember when he'd last moved so freely and easily and couldn't. For as long as he could remember--and, strangely, his memory went no further back than his own induction into the Knights of the Trinity--he had worn the silvery armor of his appointment and carried the sword of light given to him by the Order.

 *"Armin often brags about your skill with a blade. Let's see if the tales are true. Spar with me, brother."*

Lucis blinked in surprise. Such invitations came rarely. He never did determine whether Michael honored the recipient with such a request or whether the Archangel simply used it as a ploy to assert his dominance and superiority. The

Everlasting's right-hand man gave little away, letting his masculine beauty blind his opponents and deceive them into thinking him weak or ineffectual. Lucis thought he'd never come across a stronger, more calculating being than the Archangel.

Lucis looked up. Michael raised one golden eyebrow above a sapphire eye.

"Sure, how could I refuse a chance to spar with a warrior of your fame? What was the nickname they gave you after smashing the rebellion of the First Age?".

The Archangel shook his head

 *"Aww, young Lucis. I do not revel in titles or pine after the affection of angels as I once desired. I have evolved past such nonsense. Besides, that was a long, long time ago"*

Without so much as a gesture, Michael cleared the wooded area. The turf beneath their feet remained resilient and firm, the rich scents of loam and grass rising from wherever their feet trod. The two angels faced each other. Lucis drew his shiny broadsword. Light flashed, and Michael's formerly empty hand wrapped around the hilt of his golden sword.

 "I have to learn how to do that,"

Michael chuckled, positioned himself, and raised his blade.

"Let's begin, shall we?"

 "As my lord commands."

 "Your courtesy is starting to annoy me, there is no need for such formality. Now come at me, and don't you dare hold back" Michael said with a shrug and lunged.

Blades flashed and whirled, kissed with sharp clangs of sound and hisses of sliding metal. Both opponents stepped lightly upon their makeshift sparring grounds. Except for the clash of blades, eerie silence cloaked the fight. Lucis struggled to hold his own against the superior strength and bladesmanship of the Archangel, as he knew he would. But he fought with cunning and strategy countering Michael's never-ending onslaught of fluid attacks.

 "Not bad. Not bad. Perhaps Armin did not exaggerate your talents as he does the rest of the lot," Michael complimented, showing neither shortness of breath nor fatigue.

Lucis, pressed forward with confidence. Perhaps age had gotten the better of his master. Michael's lips curved into a smile. Or maybe that was a sneer. And Lucis understood. Michael had been toying with him. The Knight's self-assurance shattered as he was overwhelmed by a wicked flurry of swordsmanship that took his breath away, not to mention his broadsword. As far as he could remember, no one had ever been able to dislodge his sword from his mighty grip. Michael had gotten the better of him; he knew he could not prevail against the Archangel's superior skill, but perhaps his cunning could still win the day. Ducking beneath the swipe of a razor edge by a hair's breadth, Lucis rolled to his sword, positioned himself on one knee, and plunged his massive, jewel-encrusted broadsword into the ground. Blinding white light exploded and filled the clearing. It surprised Michael, causing him to falter just enough for Lucis to gain the advantage. Lucis yanked his sword from the ground and lunged in one swift move.

"Do you yield?" he gasped; the point of his blade held to the Archangel's throat.

Michael's gaze flickered down the length of the silvery blade. He raised his hands to the sky and smiled, an expression of astonishment upon his face. *"Using your divine power just to best me in a sparring match. Interesting? Clearly you don't like to lose, eh choir boy."*

"I say again: do you yield?" Lucis asked and steadied his hold on the sword.

"And what if I don't" Michael said curtly, *"What do you intend to do when MY power is unleashed?"*

AS SOON AS THE WORDS OF WARNING WERE SPOKE, MICHAEL'S PHYSICAL PRESENCE TRANSFORMED. ALL THE COLORS OF THE RAINBOW, AN AWESOME SIGHT TO BEHOLD. ALL KNIGHTS COLOR CHANGED WHEN THE USED THE SOURCE OF THEIR STRENGTH, BUT TO TURN EVERY COLOR THE EVERLASTING CREATED; THIS WAS LIKE NOTHING LUCIS HAD EVER WITNESSED BEFORE. THE GROUND AROUND THEM BEGAN TO TREMBLE, ROCKS STARTED COMING UP FROM THE EARTH BELOW. MICHAEL WAS TAPPING INTO HIS POWER, AN AWESOME POWER THAT MADE LUCIS SHOW OF STRENGTH LOOK LIKE A MERE MAGICIAN'S TRICK. Beads of sweat ran down Lucis's cheeks.

Fine mess I got myself into, if I show weakness, he may kill me, but if I continue to press...

Michael could taste the fear in his sparring partner. He had his fun making Lucis sweat, there was no reason to continue the charade. Michael closed his eyes gently, the ground ceased to move, and the earth was now still as it obeyed the will of its master.

"I yield" said Michael loudly, *"Why not? After all it was just a spar between friends, right?"*

Lucis quickly dropped the broadsword and stood in silence. He did not want to antagonize the situation any further. Besides, what do you say when someone has just clearly spared your life for the sheer enjoyment of watching you squirm.

Michael slapped Lucis on the back...hard.

 "Well done, Lucis. I am impressed with tenacity and will to win. No knight has ever bested me in combat, not even, Armin. I guess I underestimated you."

Lucis replied, cautiously. *"No offense, Michael, but I believe the others don't have the stomach to fight you for real."*

 "You're probably right. But they don't fear me; they fear my legend, my position, my charge as the Archangel, their leader."

"I would say after my experience today, their fears are accurate"

 "Perhaps"

Lucis sighed and shook his head.

Without any discernible gesture or word, the world around them conformed to Michael's will. A table and two chairs sprouted from the Eon, all smooth, gleaming stone. A pitcher and two glasses materialized on the tabletop.

"Have a drink with me, Lucis the Lightbringer. We have much to discuss."

Lucis complied and took a seat. He assumed the duty of the host and poured for both. Unlike his usual subtle, twisted manner, Michael wasted no time with prevarication.

"Do you know what I am wearing?"

"No, I can't say that I do"

"This is called a dreamcoat. The same dreamcoat given to King Jacob in the year 723 BC. A gift from his father, to show that he favored Jacob, his youngest son, above all his brothers."

Lucis looked puzzled *"Is that so? I have never bothered to notice what human wear. All I see is good and evil deeds"*

Michael sighed

"I figured I would hear that from one of those imbeciles out there, but not from you. I have observed you on Eon, you seem to care about humans more than you will admit"

"I think there is truth to that. There is a lot to be said about the human race, they have their faults, but they can be very kind and loving as well. I have witnessed it"

"Yes, and the fact that you acknowledge it puts you head and shoulders above the rest of the lot. Humans are a fascinating species. I have studied them for centuries and they always do something new that excites me"

"Wow, Michael. I never seen you this animated before" "Who knew it is human beings that sparked your interest?"

"Yes. I care for them dearly, and that is why I summoned you here to speak with me" Michael face changed from glee to dismay.

"I am concerned that the realms of men will fall and fall soon"

"What? Why?"

"The fate of humanity grows ever darker, viler and more sinful. The race descends further into destruction. They've doomed themselves and the planets they have dominion over."

"They have their faults, but it is still good in mankind. I see it every day. We just need to give them more time; they are still a very young species."

"Yes, yes, humankind has many good examples," Michael said, dismissing them with a wave of his hand. "But their many transgressions have unleashed an evil I fear that even the Order cannot defeat."

"What evil? Name it, and I will seek it out directly."

"I fear that an ancient evil, a demon from the first age has returned to the realms of men. I can feel his presence. And it is gaining strength every day, feeding on the sins of wicked."

Lucis set down his glass and held his silence, contemplating the truly awful circumstance of one of the terrible beasts of the Old Testament descending to Eon to wreak havoc upon the realm under his protection.

"This evil cannot stand, where can I find it and bring you the creature's head"

"Find it," Michael echoed, smirking. "It has been lurking on Planet Eon for the past two years, hiding right under your nose. Your divided attention to the choir and your realm has left planet Eon vulnerable. Instead of worrying about the squabbling of a tone-deaf angels, you have forgotten your true charge: eradicating demons trying to take over the realm you protect. I planned our little encounter to remind you. Think of it as a subtle nudge in the right direction."

"Thank you, Michael. I will rectify this at once. Can you handle the choir while I am away?"

"Certainly, I would be happy to, but face this evil alone! Are you sure? You know I cannot assist you, as I am not allowed to visit the realms of men for another century. Be patient, Lucis, and perhaps we can defeat this filth together."

"I cannot wait that long. Too many people will perish. The risk is too great. With your permission, I would like to return to Eon now. I must act quickly to save my planet."

"Of course. You face adversity head on, guns blazing. Besides, based on our little sparring session, I couldn't stop you even if I wanted to." Michael favored him with a small smile of appreciation for the Knight's tenacity.

"Go forth against evil, Lucis the Lightbringer, and may the Everlasting be with you always"

"May the Everlasting be with you as well Michael."

Lucis vanished in a bright flash of silvery light. Michael drained his glass, refilled it, and smiled.

4 We are Legion

"Your fear takes hold of you. I can smell it" - Legion

EPISODE FOUR
Lucis, Knight of the Everlasting Order, faces off against Legion, a demon from the First Age

Acrid, choking smoke filled the night air; the effect of a nearby gas tank explosion which drew cheers from the gathering crowds. Rioters filled the back streets of the city with knives, pipes, firebombs, baseball bats, and small firearms determined to bring about vigilante justice for latest calamity within a corrupt political system. Many of them held up signs that read NO BORDER LAWS, a controversial bill that declared martial law in border towns such as this one. Obviously, no one asked for these people's opinion when the bill passed that morning, and military forces started rolling in. The powers that be were prepared as well. Soldiers equipped with full riot gear hit sticks, and tear gas lined the streets, determined to push back the growing tide of protest and bring back law and order. The two forces crashed against each other. Fists, blood, and teeth flew as both sides took heavy losses. Cars were overturned, stores looted, and the building was set ablaze. Chaos and sin gripped the city with no end in sight to the growing conflict. From his perch, Legion smiled. His beady eyes, jet black complexion, and slender frame blended in with the night sky. The demon feasted upon the sumptuous banquet of anger, violence, and chaos unfolding before him. His insatiable appetite relished the evil excesses of humans who only seemed too willing to cater to it. It amused him to know that he had God to thank for humanity's gift of free will. That gift made his work such a pleasure. His efforts to stoke the simmering resentments of those who considered themselves oppressed bore such sweet fruit.

It didn't take much. A few whispers here, some rumors there, shouts of violence and hatred organized into stirring slogans.

With thousands engaged in the conflict, Legion merely plucked from the crowd those whose extra-dark souls were ripe for consumption. It was not like they could see him. An ancient demon of the ancient world, his presence could be felt but seldom witnessed by human eyes--a trick he took full advantage of. Like a fancy lady picking sweets off a silver tray, long fingers extending from cadaverous hands snatched human delicacies off streets and sidewalks. He revealed his hideous, demonic figure to them just to extract that last sweet bit of terror from their essence as he feasted. To Legion, that was the best part: watching their reaction as he brought them into his flesh and sucked their corrupted souls

from their bodies until they were nothing more than globs of melted goo that could be scraped off the bottom of one's shoe. With each sun-drenched soul, he devoured, his power and strength increased.

Their terror and pain only sweetened the flavor of their condemned souls.

A booming voice behind him interrupted his sweet, sweet banquet.

"This is my realm and you are trespassing. Begone, demon, you have no authority here" the angel's voice intoned.

Legion paid no mind to the distraction and finished his meal.

He wiped the drool from his mouth and turned to deal with this distraction. He smiled when he gazed upon his adversary. Drool dripped in a steady stream to the pavement below, sizzling where it splattered.

"Drauta dom shen la mocasca sinufa, Yuckas."

"Do not speak to me as if I were one of your minions, demon! I will not dare converse in your accursed tongue on this realm, or any other for that matter!"

With a blur of speed, Legion plucked another rioting human from the crowd and consumed him. The angel's eyes narrowed behind his silvery helm, and his hand tightened upon the hilt of his broadsword. Discarding the melted carcass, Legion spoke

"Sin. Sin gives me authority. These men are ripe with it"

"Stay your foul tongue, beast. Say no more, lest I remove your head from your body."

Seventh Spark - Knights of the Trinity

"Hehehehe" Legion leaned closer to Lucis and gave him a toothless grin, thick viscous saliva flowing from his mouth and sizzling like acid where it landed.

A gaunt face, hideous and menacing, protruded from Legion's chest. It snapped serrated teeth at Lucis, ravening hunger gleaming in its hollow eyes. Lucis jumped back, startled and unnerved by the implications.

The demon's face twisted in a dreadful snarl as he pressed his son's look back into the prison of his body. Legion continued to speak.

"Forgive. My children hunger for your essence. The sweetest meat, so tasty"

A lump lodged in the angel's throat. With dismay, Lucis recognized it as fear. He swallowed and summoned a burst of bravado. Thumping an armored fist against his silver breastplate, he replied,

"I am an anointed warrior for God. There is no sin here for your feasting."

"Fear, your fear smells sweet" Legion licked his lips, inhaled deeply, and smiled. Drool hissed where it hit the concrete. He wiped his mouth and flung the slobber aside. Five gaunt faces pressed through the demon's skin, snapping their pointed teeth and shrieking with hunger. They clamored for a taste of Lucis. The angel did not miss the panic that flickered across the demon's face as he forced his offspring back inside his body.

One of them broke free of his grasp and shot forward, lunging toward the angel. It's clutching, skeletal hands and serrated teeth came within a hair's breadth of him. Lucis took a giant step backward. His foot slipped on the goo from Legion's last meal, and he fell to the ground. He gazed in horror at the grisly splotches of human remains festering on the pavement.

Legion had been busy. This demon was different than one's Lucis had encountered in the past; they were fierce, but this one... this one shook him to his core. Lucis stood up quickly, trying his best to hide the terror growing inside of him. He shook the disgusting goo off his hands and prepared himself for the worst. Reluctantly, he drew his massive broadsword and prepared for battle.

The sight of his reaction made Legion chuckle, drool spewing from his toothless maw.

"Young one. Foolish and quick to action. Just like the other."

"What other?" Lucis shouted *"There are no other angels on this realm"*

Legion chuckled once more

"Hehehehe. I am not bound to your rules, I come and go as I please. You know little. I was once a Knight of the Everlasting, a puppet playing Michael's game, just like you" Lucis had had enough.

"No more talking, demon. Your foul breath poisons the air. I will entertain no more of your lies and deceit. Prepare yourself, demon, for you die today!"

Legion chuckled and reached for the weapon slung across his back. He hefted an ancient, double-headed ax with dark runes etched into both sides of the blades. Faces, each in a rictus of terror, pressed against the surface from inside the shaft. There were many to be seen. Too many to count. All languishing in agony from inside the demonic weapon of the old age. They served as a warning to anyone who dared face Legion.

Lucis did his best to stand firm but could not help looking away. Legion took notice of his cowardice and pressed his advantage.

"Fear, your fear takes hold of you...I can smell it. You are in my world now, and in my world, darkness is light."

In a blink of an eye, the world around Lucis changed. Time and space stood still as darkness surrounded them. The chaos of the ongoing conflict and cries of human suffering vanished as if hidden by some invisible veil. The battle between light and darkness, good and evil, Lucis and Legion would be shrouded in secrecy, the black of night, just as the demon intended.

Furious, Lucis interrupted.

"Enough of your tricks! We all know that the dark can never defeat the light."

Legion's chuckled, wiped the ooze dripping from his mouth, then twisted the hilt of his weapon to face Lucis.

"Hehehehe. You know little, young one. See for yourself"

Lucis gasped. He recognized that the face and the soul trapped inside the great-ax: Artemus, the Protector.

"Ahhhh!"

LUCIS SCREAMED AS HE SWUNG HIS MIGHTY BROADSWORD, DETERMINED TO SPLIT LEGION IN TWO. THE DEMON EASILY AVOIDED THE ATTACK AND TOOK THE OFFENSIVE. LACKING THE SHEER BRUTE STRENGTH TO MATCH THE MIGHTY KNIGHT, HIS QUICK, UNPREDICTABLE MOVEMENTS EVADED THE ANGEL'S STRIKES. THE ANGEL'S USUALLY PRECISE BLADE WORK GREW SLOPPY. LEGION'S ACROBATIC SPEED DODGED EACH ATTACK. HIS GAPING, DRIPPING MAW STRETCHED INTO A SLY GRIN, TASTING THE FEAR AND RAGE LUCIS EXPENDED WITH EVERY WILD SWING.

GRITTING HIS TEETH, LUCIS REGROUPED AND BEGAN TO CIRCLE THE DEMON. BEHIND THE SILVERY GLEAM OF HIS VISOR, HIS EYES NARROWED. THEIR WEAPONS CLASHED, A FLURRY OF FLASHING METAL AND EERIE SILENCE NEITHER SEEN NOR HEARD BY THE RIOTING HUMANS NEARBY.

LUCIS CHARGED, FINALLY GETTING INSIDE LEGION'S DEFENSES AND THE CONSISTENT PARRIES FROM HIS AX. THE ADVANCE WAS QUICKLY THWARTED AS LEGION'S CHILDREN CAME TO HIS AID, SNAPPING AND CLAWING AT LUCIS, GOUGING HIS STRONG METAL ARMOR UNTIL HE HAD NO CHOICE BUT TO RETREAT. FOR ALL THE POWER AND MIGHT, LUCIS POSSESSED, LEGION

APPEARED UNTOUCHABLE. WITH A PERFECT STRIKE, THE DEMON SLASHED LUCIS ACROSS THE CHEST, PIERCING THE SHINING ARMOR. THE ANGEL RETREATED, GROANING IN AGONY.

LEGION GAVE A QUICK SIGH OF RELIEF AT THE MOMENT'S RESPITE. THE PAUSE ALLOWED HIM TIME TO GET HIS CHILDREN BACK UNDER CONTROL. THE CONSTANT STRUGGLE FOR POWER BETWEEN HIM AND HIS OFFSPRING WAS BEGINNING TO TAKE ITS TOLL, ALTHOUGH LEGION HID IT WELL.

LUCIS TOOK A RUNNING LEAP AT LEGION. HE RAISED HIS SWORD OVER HIS HEAD FOR ONE FINAL BLOW, A BLOW LEGION DODGED WITH LITTLE DIFFICULTY. THE SWORD PIERCED THE CONCRETE BENEATH THEIR FEET AND SANK INTO THE GROUND BELOW.

Legion started to laugh, spraying drool.

"You know little. My skill exceeds yours. You cannot prevail."

From behind his helm, Lucis' mouth curled in a small smile.

"I wasn't trying to hit you."

A FLASH OF BLINDING LIGHT ILLUMINATED THE ENTIRE CITY. THE BLAST OF PURE LIGHT NOT ONLY BLINDED LEGION BUT ALSO THE THOUSANDS OF RIOTERS AND SOLDIERS ENGAGED IN THE CONFLICT AROUND THEM. EVERYONE AND EVERYTHING STOPPED TO TAKE NOTICE OF SUCH AN IMPRESSIVE SIGHT.

LEGION CRINGED AND DROPPED TO HIS KNEES, SCREAMING IN AGONY AS SMOKE WAFTED FROM HIS SCORCHED BODY. HIS CHILDREN CRIED OUT IN ECHO OF THEIR FATHER'S PAIN AND RETREATED INTO LEGION'S BODY FOR RELIEF. BLISTERS ERUPTED ALL OVER HIS SINGED FLESH.

PUS OOZED, AND BOILS BURST FROM THE HOLY LIGHT'S EXTREME HEAT. THE MIGHTY LEGION WAS OVERCOME BY THE POWER OF THE EVERLASTING BLISTERING LIGHT. HE STAGGERED TO HIS FEET AND EXAMINED HIS HANDS IN SHOCK. THEY WERE SMOKING, BLACK, GNARLED, AND BLISTERED. HE HOWLED AGAIN IN ANGUISH. LUCIS TOOK ADVANTAGE OF THE DEMON'S DISTRACTION. HE SNEAKED BEHIND LEGION AND CLAMPED HIS ARMS AROUND THE BEAST IN A BRUTAL SQUEEZE, CAUSING HIM TO DROP THE BATTLE-AX.

LUCIS GLANCED AGAIN AT HIS SWORD, ITS HOLY LIGHT DIMMED.

THE LIGHT BLINDED THE CROWDS OF PEOPLE RIOTING IN STREETS AROUND THEM, AN EFFECT THAT SURPRISED BOTH COMBATANTS. ONCE THE BRILLIANCE SUBSIDED, BOTH LEGION AND LUCIS WERE REVEALED.

Seventh Spark - Knights of the Trinity

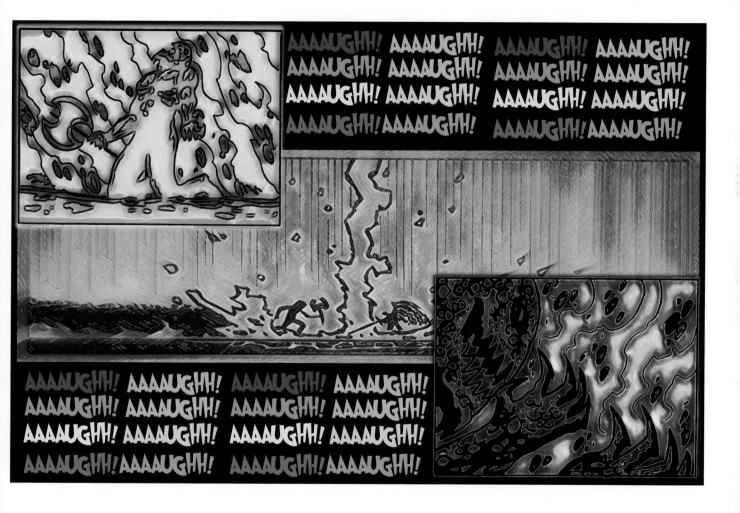

Thousands of people crowded close to see the spectacle, rioters, and military alike. News crews were on the scene, and helicopters hovered in the sky. The world was watching now. Was it real, or was this an elaborate movie or demonstration? No one knew or cared; they just knew whatever was happening was special. This will be my finest hour, Lucis thought. Armin once warned him that shining God's light from inside him would cost him his life, but Lucis did not care. Lodged deep into the earth, his sword was no use to him anyway.

He was honored to give his life if it meant defeating such an ancient and powerful evil. Better yet, he had the chance to do it in front of thousands of people. Perhaps his sacrifice would turn mankind from their wicked ways. Lucis threw his head back, closed his eyes, and let out a victory scream as thousands looked on in anticipation. He envisioned the holy light consuming him and his enemy in a glorious blaze of brilliance. Only... his brilliant glow did not come.

He concentrated harder and tried again, arms gripped tightly around Legion. Once again, nothing.

Still smoking and in pain, Legion blurted,

"Ahh...it burns, it burns us"

"Quiet, demon,"

Lucis snarled as he reached for the divine power lurking within him. It danced out of reach, frustrating the Knight.

Legion guessed at the angel's dilemma and chuckled.

"Hehehehe. You know little"

"Know what?"

Lucis grunted as he dug deeply for his suddenly elusive gift.

"You have limits young one. Your gift can only be used only once in battle"

"You lie! How would you know that?"

"I was once like you, the Everlasting's pet. Morningstar showed me a power without limits, without controls, unlike Michael who hoards all power and control to himself."

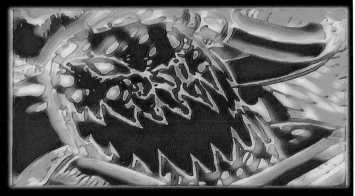

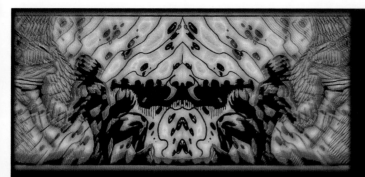

"Liar!"

"Hehehehe. You know little. Your light dims. Can you feel it?"

The demon laughed and bucked against the armored arms encasing him.

Lucis felt himself weaken. Was Legion telling the truth, or were the demon's manipulation and darkness confusing him? Lucis began to panic. He was losing power quickly, and the whole world watched. He could not let evil triumph, yet he could not stop it. At least he had battled Legion to a stalemate: that had to count for something. Unable to free himself from Lucis' hold, Legion's anguish turned to anger. He could not bear humiliation at the hands of such an inadequate opponent.

"You know little, young one. Your lust for glory will unleash a dark evil that even I fear. My offspring are vile, wretched things, a base evil not meant for this world. I contained them to keep balance between good and evil, but I can no longer contain these festering aberrations in my weakened state."

The demon howled in anguish,

"My children, be free."

THE GROUND CRUMBLED BENEATH LEGION'S FEET, OPENING A HOLE THAT SPEWED FIRE AND LAVA. LUCIS RELEASED HIS GRASP ON THE DEVIL AND JUMPED BACK TO AVOID FALLING INTO THE BURNING PIT, BUT NOTHING COULD PREPARE HIM FOR WHAT HE WITNESSED NEXT.

ONE BY ONE, LEGIONS CHILDREN CRAWLED OUT HIS BODY AS ANCIENT DEMON SCREAMED IN EXCRUCIATING PAIN, THEIR EMANCIPATION LEAVING HIM HOLLOW AND WEAK. IN THE END, FIVE INDIVIDUAL HORRORS STOOD OVER HIM AS LEGION FELL TO HIS KNEES AT THE EDGE OF THE FIERY PIT. EACH NEW DEMON BORE DISTINCT PHYSICAL ATTRIBUTES AND SIZE; ALL BORE SOME RESEMBLANCE TO THEIR FATHER.

LEGION CRUMPLED. LYING PRONE ON THE GROUND, HE LOOKED UP AT THE DARKNESS HE HAD SPAWNED. NO FOOL, HE KNEW THE HORROR HE HAD UNLEASHED AND WHAT IT MEANT FOR HIM. GAZING AT THEM, HE NAMED THE SONS WHO HOVERED NEAR HIM, DROOLING WITH RAVENOUS HUNGER: PAIN, CHAOS, FEAR, DECEIT, AND PRIDE. PROPER NAMES FOR CHILDREN OF THE DAMMED, LEGION THOUGHT. HE SMILED WITH SATISFACTION. HIS WORK WAS DONE. LEGION CLOSED HIS EYES, AT PEACE WITH THE HORROR HE'D WROUGHT.

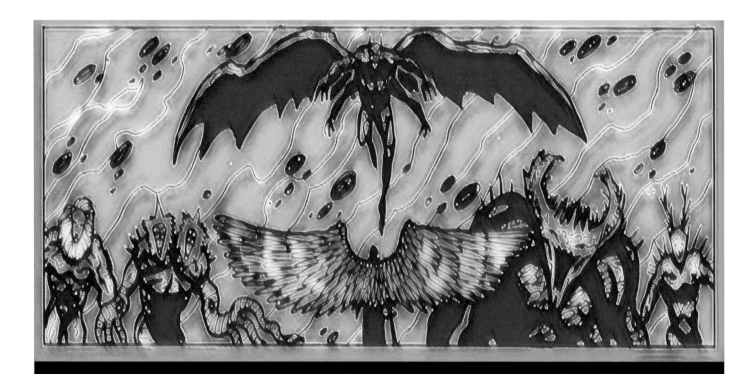

PRIDE DECIET FEAR CHAOS PAIN

The five starving demons wasted no time ripping into Legion's flesh to feast on him. Their father neither struggled nor fought. Without so much as a whimper, he let his children consume him as he knew they would. The five demons gorged on his flesh and the evil power stored inside, each howling in delight.

The crowd became uneasy. Spectacle, performance, or nothing of the sort, most of the people thought it an excellent time to leave, just in case what they witnessed was real. Some stayed close, determined to see this horror to its grisly end.

Perhaps, they thought, the angel with the big sword would protect them.

Lucis regained his sword, but not his fighting spirit or his confidence. His light was fading fast. He could not beat one ancient demon; now, there were five. He could not, in good conscience, simply abandon the scene, so he considered one final plan of attack. The demons were still devouring their father; perhaps he could sneak up behind them and,

One demon's ears perked up as if it heard Lucis' thoughts.

It turned its head and hissed at Lucis with a forked tongue.

Alerted, all the brothers stood up to face the angel together. The largest one in the middle spoke in a deep, dark voice: *"We are free because of you"* *"Leave now or be devoured."*

The demon flapped his massive leathery wings and rose into the air, hovering over the pit. The other demons prepared themselves for battle, all drooling in anticipation.

Lucis' heart pounded; his hands grew icy. A cold sweat trickled down his back as a new sensation washed over him. He had never felt something like this before. What was it? What should he do? The demon bat's smile widened, and it shouted one word, *"Fear!"*

"No,"

Lucis grunted and took a step backward. The demon paused, momentarily surprised by the angel's retreat. Acting on instinct, Lucis called once again for his power of light. It did not respond to his summons.

Seventh Spark - Knights of the Trinity Saga

His fist closed over the hilt of his sword. Perhaps he could defeat them the old-fashioned way--and lose his life in the effort.

He wondered if Artemus had sacrificed himself to save his realm from Legion. Surely, there was a better way?

Sensing the Knight's indecision, the demon bat's hoarse voice filled the air with a low, grating chuckle. Its cadaverous throat uttered a single word: *"Kill."*

The demon named Pain picked up Legion's battle ax and hefted it with an effortless skill reminiscent of his father's. Outnumbered and afraid of the sacrifice, Lucis flew into the night, filled with fear and shame.

"Coward!" the demon bat taunted, pointing and laughing. It turned its empty white eyes to its brothers and said, *"Feast."* Hiding on top of a high-rise building, Lucis watched helplessly and in shame as Legion's sons loosed themselves upon the unsuspecting crowd. He waited, curious to see what the power of men could do against such reckless evil.

ON THE GROUND, PEOPLE JOINED IN DEFIANCE OF A COMMON ENEMY. THEY BELIEVED NOTHING COULD MATCH THE WILLPOWER AND SHEER FORCE OF MEN AND THEIR WEAPONS. LOUD ORDERS BOOMED AS GUNFIRE PIERCED THE NIGHT AIR. TEAR GAS AND SMOKE BOMBS FOGGED THE SKY. THOUSANDS HELD BATS, CLUBS, AND KNIVES TO KEEP THE DEMONS AT BAY. ALL THEIR EFFORTS PROVED FUTILE AS THE HORRIBLE SOUNDS OF BEASTS PREVAILED, GORGING THEMSELVES ON HUMAN SOULS AND LEAVING PUDDLES OF HUMAN GOO IN THEIR WAKE.

THE DEMONS HUNTED DOWN PEACEKEEPERS AND RIOTERS ALIKE. TO THEM, ONLY FEAR AND SIN MATTERED, NOT WHATEVER SIDE OF THE BORDER THEY WERE ON OR THEIR POLITICAL AFFILIATION. THEY FEASTED UPON A BUFFET OF EVIL AND CHAOS. IN THE END, ONLY POOLS OF FESTERING GOO REMAINED.

LUCIS HUNG HIS HEAD IN DISGUST, ASHAMED OF HIS PRIDE, HIS FEAR, AND HIS COWARDICE. THE BRILLIANT WHITE LIGHT THAT ALWAYS SURROUNDED HIM FADED AS HE FLED INTO THE NIGHT SKY.

Episode Four

5 | Immortals

"Lucis, you shame us"– Stevyn

Stevyn the Beast, smirked at the wrinkled noses of the humans whom he passed unseen. Garbed in his usual barbaric array of massive animal skins, he left a pungent odor of rotting hides and old sweat trailing in his wake. The sour smell of Rupin, his sabretooth cat and constant companion added to puzzled looks and disgusted expressions.

Although how the city's denizens living in urban squalor could distinguish the odors from the overpowering stench of smoke, unwashed flesh, open sewage, and automotive exhaust, he had no idea. Really, humans were such filthy creatures.

As he prowled the crowded, twisting alleys and lanes winding around ramshackle cookshops, drug dens, brothels, merchants, and residences of a densely populated slum in Duskdale, Stevyn searched for his brother-in-arms--oh, what was that nasty brown puddle of sludge he just stepped in?-- The din of human noise made him long for the vast, wild spaces of his own realm where the wind blew clean, and herds of beasts roamed at will. He wondered at Lucis' silence; it worried him. He and Lucis were close, Stevyn took his silence as a slight. Something was wrong, and it was past time to find out just what was going on. The angel chuckled to himself, imagining Jewel's reaction to navigating this cesspool of human habitation. If Armin had sent her to check up on Lucis, she'd never let him hear the end of it.

That was probably why his appointed leader assigned him the errand. The other Knights were just too persnickety. He sighed, which meant he first inhaled, which meant that he coughed on the stench of poverty-stricken urban squalor. Shrieks of high-pitched laughter, shouts, and yells of anger and commerce, and occasional (and ignored) screams of fear and pain pierced the slum. Stevyn's keen ears heard the meaty thud of fists on flesh and the feminine cry that followed.

That shriek came from a young girl, too young to ignore"

he muttered to himself, smiled with predatory anticipation, and headed inside the brothel. Still un-seen by the throngs of filthy humanity, he took no notice of those whom he shoved aside nor of their reactions when they accused one another of rude behavior and fell to fisticuffs to defend their nonexistent honor. Single-minded intensity suffused him as he charged forward to rid the universe of a soul-drenched in evil. Stevyn flung open the heavy curtain that served as a door, tearing the curtain rod from its moorings with a clatter. He took only a second to ascertain that he had the correct room: a bruised and bleeding girl beneath the rutting beast of a man twice her weight. The Knight's meat-hook of a hand grabbed the girl's un-pleasant customer around the throat and yanked him off her.

He squeezed his fist, smiling as the human spine cracked and compressed beneath the force of his grip. He tossed the twitching body aside; it thudded against the flimsy wall and slid to the floor in a fleshy, stinking heap. The girl scrambled backward, blood staining her pale, skinny thighs.

Stevyn glanced at the girl and felt the burn of rage and a deep swell of grief. Too young. She was too damn young, still a child. Where in the hell was Lucis? He was supposed to prevent such evil, or at least rescue the victims of it. He revealed himself and extended his hands toward her, but she shrank back in terror, the wordless gibbering of fear dribbling from her lips. He tried smiling, but that didn't help. He closed his lips, concealing the sharp points of his teeth. That didn't help much, either.

The girl squeaked as Rupin materialized beside her. Her eyes grew wide as she whimpered. But the enormous saber-toothed cat merely nuzzled her, rubbing the broad flat area between his ears against the girl's body and--was that damned cat purring? The sound apparently had the desired effect of soothing the girl's fear. She relaxed and even dared to rub her small hands over the ferocious beast. Rupin blinked his yellow-green eyes at Stevyn in feline superiority as though to say, *"Chump."* Stevyn shook his head in wry amusement. Cursing Lucis under his breath,

Stevyn laid his hands on the battered, violated girl to expend a smidgen of his vast power and heal her wounded spirit, spilling a soothing balm upon her mind and soul. The physical injuries would have to heal naturally. He prayed she would avoid the that would likely see her dead before she reached mature adulthood. After a moment, he finished and straightened to his full height, the top of his head brushing the ceiling. Rupin nuzzled the girl one more time and then glanced at the carcass. The cat sniffed at the lump of dead flesh and turned up his nose in feline distaste. Stevyn didn't blame the cat for not wanting to take a bite of the sweaty, stinking carcass. His rage returned, sparking an answering growl from the cat.

 "Leave here and never come back."

Her eyes widened with terror. She did not understand a word he said, but the tone of voice came through loud and clear. She gathered her ragged dress around herself and bolted.

Fading into invisibility again, Stevyn, the Beast, turned on his heel and stomped back through the building, his cat following close behind. He spared a moment to wonder if the girl would find herself in better circumstances, then dismissed the concern from his mind. The humans in this realm were Lucis' responsibility, not his.

Finally, he found the object of his search and found himself appalled and disappointed at the once-mighty warrior before him.

 "Really? I come all this way only to find you like this? How has the mighty Lightbringer been reduced to hiding in the shadows?"

Fitting into his environment with uncanny accuracy, the old Chinese drunkard opened his bleary eyes and took a swig from a nearly empty bottle. He belched and scratched his balls. Rupin growled. Stevyn felt like growling, too.

 "Lucis, you shame us."

Disguised as the lowest of the low in that squalid slum, Lucis took another gulp from the bottle and drained it. He flung it aside, not reacting when the glass crashed and shattered, not caring when an old woman glared at him and shouted curses.

 "Two whole years, no word, not one word. Not even to me, your best friend. Your entire realm is falling apart, and you just wallow here covered in piss and shit. That's fine behavior for a Knight."

"Fuck off, Stevyn. I am not in the mood for your lecture."

Lucis muttered and belched...again.

And where was the slacker, anyway? Why wasn't he protecting the weak and nurturing the good? What happened to his friend and valiant warrior?

The Knight returned to prowling the Chinese slum, resolutely ignoring the abject poverty and open displays of sin. Determined to carry out his assignment as efficiently as possible, he shoved people aside, knocked down market carts, and broke through walls to reach his quarry. The angry shouts of protest he left in his wake did not trouble him at all.

He held out his hand, and a full bottle of whatever liquor he favored appeared in his grasp. With his upper lip curled in a sneer, he threw it at Stevyn. Another full bottle appeared in his hand. With an inebriated efficiency born of steady practice, the angel twisted off the cap and tossed it aside. He lifted the bottle to his mouth and guzzled. He scratched himself again with his free hand.

 "Armin's worried about you. So am I."

Lucis belched. Liquor dribbled from his mouth. Not for the first time did he think that men were wrong: liquor did not imbue a man with forgetfulness. The memories always came back, as did the shame. But still, it worked better than anything else he had tried.

 "I had to ask for permission,"

Steven added, lips screwing and nose wrinkling in an expression of extreme distaste. He crouched, leaning into his once-proud brother-in-arms.

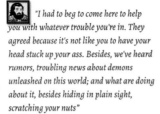 *"I had to beg to come here to help you with whatever trouble you're in. They agreed because it's not like you to have your head stuck up your ass. Besides, we've heard rumors, troubling news about demons unleashed on this world; and what are doing about it, besides hiding in plain sight, scratching your nuts"*

Lucis snorted and took another swig, not in the least interested in whatever futile task anyone assigned to him.

 "I said, FUCK OFF!"

 "What happened to you?"

Stevyn asked, concerned that whatever had reduced his once-mighty brother-in-arms to such a low state would affect the rest of the Knights. Lucis answered him with another belch, scratch, and guzzle.

Stevyn had seen and heard enough, he decided to let his fist do the talking. One clean shot to the jaw with his massive left hand was all it took. The warrior Knight turned street vagrant was unconscious laying in his own piss and filth.

Stevyn plucked his friend off the street. Slinging over his shoulder the remains of what had once been the most admirable of their company, he transported them to a secluded place high in the austere, windswept mountains of Tibet. The monks of the small Tibetan monastery he commandeered never knew why they obeyed a strange compulsion to flee their sanctuary, but they never returned it. He chuckled to himself, remembering the show he put on in their collective dreams, assuming the frightening visage of a vengeful warrior god of pagan belief, shaking his fists and shouting at them to leave.

 "You stink,"

Stevyn exclaimed as he dunked Lucis into a bottom-less barrel of cold water.

 "You are already sulking like a human, do you have to smell like them as well?"

Lucis came up, sputtering. Stevyn cared not as he dunked his brother again. And again. When Stevyn decided he'd shocked Lucis sufficiently into coherence, he forced hot porridge down his throat.

 "You'll fill your belly with something else besides alcohol, you pitiful sot,"

he growled, barely waiting until Lucis swallowed before wrenching his jaw open again to force-feed him another spoonful of gruel.

He followed the coarse meal with another round of dunking in icy cold water.

"Enough!"

Lucis shouted and wrested himself from Stevyn's hands.

"Give me one good reason why I shouldn't beg--beg--Michael to revoke your status as a Knight?"

Ever at his side, Rupin growled and hissed, displaying fearsome teeth.

 "You humiliate yourself."

"I failed!"

Lucis spat. Shivering, arms wrapped around himself, he turned a look of self-pity upon the other Knight and repeated in a sullen tone,

"I failed."

 "That happens, you dolt. Or have you forgotten?"

"You don't understand!"

Stevyn sighed and took a seat. "Then why don't you explain it to me?"

Sniveling and shivering and too

weak to manifest his angelic form, Lucis plopped to the cold, hard floor. He wiped his runny nose on the back of the wet, dirty sleeve, ignoring Stevyn's look of disgust. He took a deep breath, one of surprising sobriety, and spoke. He used small words, short sentences. He related only the barest facts of his confrontation with Legion and his failure to vanquish him. He revealed the release of Legion's demon sons into the world and how he could do nothing to prevent it.

"I failed."

 "Yes, we established that already, please continue,"

Stevyn agreed with his characteristic lack of tact.

"Even worse, I feared."

 "And, so, humans frighten me all time, creepy little buggers, ain't that right Rupin?"

Rupin nodded in agreement with his master.

"What? No, this has nothing to do with humans. I was scared of; I was scared of a demon."

Stevyn looked puzzled, as he raised an eyebrow,

 "Are you serious? You must be joking. Our entire brotherhood is built on killing demons and eradicating evil. For real, tell me what is really bothering you?"

"I am serious, you jackass. Trust me, I couldn't believe it either, but it happened."

Stevyn's look of concern quickly turned to elation

 *"Hahahahaha! You, Lucis the Almighty Lightbringer, Master of the Broad-sword and Protector of the Eon, scared of a demon. Wow! Wait till I tell Galdy and Jewel about this one. You will never live this one down. I guess spending all that time at choir recitals has made you weak, brother."*

Lucis's eyes welled up with tears, that was the moment Stevyn realized that his friend was in real need. Stevyn wiped the tear from his left cheek and replied softly,

 "Tell me what happened Lucis, I am here for you brother."

Lucis took a few moments to compose himself, inhaled deeply, then replied,

"The demon called itself Legion, it said it was from the First Age, it even knew Michael."

Stevyn nodded, keeping his feelings of disbelief to himself,

 "Go on, I am listening."

"This was an evil, I have never faced before, he fought with such grace and elegance, my skill with a blade did nothing to counter his elusiveness, it was if the creature moved at the speed of light itself. Then those faces, those horrible faces, gnawing, biting, lunging at me, how can a demon have other demons inside of it. I mean..."

"Wait, brother, did you say a demon who carried other demons inside of it?"

"Yes, five demons, to be exact."

Stevyn hung his head and placed his hand over his chin as if in deep thought. There was something familiar about the yarn that Lucis spun, although he could not recall the memory. He decided to bang his head up against the wall until the moment rushed back to him was the best approach. Rupin rolled his eyes at the notion then curled up in a tight knot resting by the fire.

"Raguel the Archangel!"

he shouted, smiling that

headbanging method for recall did not fail him.

"You are referring to the story of Raguel the Archangel, right? Good one, brother, you almost had me believing your tall tales."

"What are you talking about?" I don't know this Raguel you speak of, and surely, he is no Archangel as there is only one Michael. Have you gone mad from the cold weather, brother?"

"You really don't know the tale, do you?" Well, Raj told it to me, so I guess it is time for me to pass it on."

Stevyn repositioned himself, found a smooth flat stone to sit on, and brought over some wood to make a fire.

"Stories like this should be told over a campfire," he told Lucis jokingly.

The Sad Tale of Raguel the Archangel

ACCORDING TO LEGEND, THE EVERLASTING CREATED SEVEN ARCHANGELS, NOT ONE. THE SEVEN WERE GIVEN TREMENDOUS POWER, RIVALING THAT OF THE EVERLASTING HIMSELF. AS THE NUMBERS OF ANGELS GREW TO INTO THE HUNDREDS OF THOUSANDS IN HEAVEN, THE SEVEN DECIDED THAT EACH OF THEM WOULD TRAIN TWELVE WARRIORS, SOLDIERS WHO COULD HANDLE THE DAY TO DAY MANAGEMENT OF THE REALM THEY LORDED OVER. EACH WARRIOR WAS PROVIDED WITH DIVINE POWER, BUT THEIR MIGHT WAS FAR INFERIOR TO THAT OF THEIR ARCHANGEL MASTERS. DURING THE WAR FOR CONTROL OF HEAVEN BETWEEN THE EVERLASTING AND LUCIFER, ANGEL FOUGHT ANGEL, BROTHER TURNED AGAINST BROTHER. STILL, NONE WERE BETRAYED MORE THAN RAGUEL, WHO WAS ATTACKED BY ALL TWELVE OF HIS KNIGHTS, THE SAME KNIGHTS SWORN TO PROTECT HIM. WHY THEY HATED HIM IS A MYSTERY, BUT IT WAS BELIEVED THAT RAGUEL POSSESSED THE RIGHTEOUSNESS OF THE EVERLASTING. PERHAPS HE RULED OVER HIS KNIGHTS TOO HARSHLY, WHO IS TO SAY, ALL THE LEGEND SPEAKS OF HIS ULTIMATE DEMISE AS HE WAS KILLED AND DRAGGED DOWN TO THE PIT OF HELL WITH THE REST OF HIS MEN. RAGUEL, THE LION, DID NOT GO DOWN WITHOUT A FIGHT THE LEGEND SAYS; HE KILLED FIVE OF HIS OWN ANGELS BEFORE THEY FINALLY OVERWHELMED HIM.

THE DEMONS DID UNSPEAKABLE THINGS TO RAGUEL IN HELL, TORTURING AND TORMENTING HIM, BUT ARCHANGEL'S RESOLVE WAS STRONG, SO STRONG HE COULD NOT BE TURNED, NOT EVEN BY LUCIFER HIMSELF. THAT WAS UNTIL HE WAS FORCED TO INHALE THE PURE ESSENCE OF THE FIVE DEMON KNIGHTS HE SLAIN IN BATTLE. THIS WAS TOO MUCH FOR RAGUEL'S SPIRIT TO BEAR, ULTIMATELY TRANSFORMING HIM INTO A GNARLED, TWISTED CREATURE, CURSED TO ENDURE TREMENDOUS PAIN AND TORMENT FROM THE SPIRITS WITHIN HIM. THEIR PLAN BACK-FIRED, AS RAGUEL WOULD NOT GIVE UP SO EASILY. HE TRAPPED THEM INTO HIS SPIRIT, HOLDING THEM CAPTIVE, CALLING UPON THEIR POWER AT HIS WILL. THE COST TO HIM WAS HIS OWN SPIRIT, AS THE SIX BEINGS BECAME ONE. IT IS SAID HE WANDERS FROM PLANET TO PLANET, DEVOURING SOULS, CONSTANTLY FEEDING, IT'S LUST TO FEED INSATIABLE, UNCONTROLLABLE, AND UNSTOPPABLE. THE FACE OF PAIN, SUFFERING AND ANGUISH CAST OUT OF BOTH HEAVEN AND HELL, CURSED TO WANDER THE REALMS OF MEN FOREVER.

"Raj believes he is more powerful than Michael himself. Of course, I didn't believe that old mystic and his grand stories of tales long past. But your story, your story about this demon, made me remember. Perhaps, the legend is true?"

Lucis pondered on the thought for a moment, then chuckled

"I have never heard such a wise tale in all my life. Raj has been inhaling too many of his own tonics again. If there were seven Archangels, we would have known about them, Armin is not one to keep secrets."

 "But what if Armin does not know? I don't know Michael well, but he does not strike me as a gossip, regaling stories from his youth."

"You can say, THAT again. That Michael is a mystery, wrapped into an enigma. However, there are too many questions that cannot be answered. Let's just keep my little discovery between you and me until I can learn more."

Stevyn nodded in agreement.

There was no need to continue to go down a rabbit hole on this one. Who or what the demon was, did not matter; what did was Lucis regaining his resolve

 "Does that mean you are ready to put your big angel britches on and get back out there?"

"Not yet. I am so ashamed. The people I swore to protect suffered and died due to my cowardice. I was too afraid to stop it."

Lucis averted his gaze and flushed with embarrassment. Never the most refined or sophisticated of their brethren, Stevyn alone bared his face to the universe and always spoke the truth. Stevyn speared him with a hard glare.

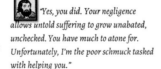 *"Yes, you did. Your negligence allows untold suffering to grow unabated, unchecked. You have much to atone for. Unfortunately, I'm the poor schmuck tasked with helping you."*

Lucis sniffed and said nothing aloud about wishing Armin had come instead. Armin would not likely beat him about the head and shoulders with brutal honesty. Stevyn, his best friend and sworn brother, would not treat him with any pretense to gentleness or even a modicum of care. He pursed his lips and decided to consider the forthcoming hardship as penance. Stevyn's heavy eyebrows lowered to form a single line across his forehead. He discerned the thoughts and worries racing through his brother's mind.

 "This isn't your penance, fool."

"Then what do you call it?"

 "Just desserts. Think of it as payback for the times you beat me sparring. Now get off your scrawny ass."

He rubbed his meaty hands together, anticipating victory over Lucis for the first time.

 *"I'm going to enjoy beating you to a pulp as much as I'm going to revel in restoring you to service."*

Days passed in the grueling physical effort as Stevyn forced Lucis to run, spar, pray, and even recite Scripture.

He battered the angel's body, mind and spirit like a blacksmith forging iron into steel, coercing him into growing stronger and ensuring he stayed sober. As Lucis strengthened and regained his skill, Rupin added his feline savagery to Stevyn's efforts, keeping the Lightbringer on his toes to restore him to the mastery he formerly command-ed.

Lucis had hardly reclaimed much of his former strength, speed, and skill with arms when Stevyn unloaded another reason for his involvement.

 "Rumor has it a mere man--a puny human--defeated one of the demons you spoke of in cave a few months ago."

"What?"

Lucis spluttered, spraying half-chewed food and feeling a renewed sense of hot shame that a human did what he could not.

 "You heard me," *"Have you no manners? Chew with your mouth closed, you cretin. And don't talk with your mouth full."*

Lucis hastily swallowed and took a large gulp of the bright, cold water drawn from the monastery's well. He demanded,

"Tell me more. I need to know."

 "If you'd been sober and attentive, you'd already know,"

Stevyn pointed out. He shrugged and winced at the hard drubbing he'd taken. Lucis had regained his fighting form. He glanced at the cat peeling flesh from the carcass of someone's missing cow. The yellow-green eyes met his and blinked. He could almost hear the cat telling him that if he were a cat, too, Lucis would never defeat them in a fight again. No one knew how to fight dirtier than a wily cat. But Lucis was talking, so he wrenched his attention away from Rupin.

"I know that. Now tell me."

 "Seems a human encountered a demon in the form a winged bat and

managed to destroy it. You--"

Not waiting for the inevitable insult, Lucis snapped,

"I need to investigate."

"Got your fighting spirit back, eh?"

"Judging by the way you and Rupin have been wincing in pain the last few days, I would say I am in good shape, wouldn't you?"

 "You can thank me later."

Stevyn rose to his feet with a heavy grunt and smile filled with pointed teeth.

 "I've taken long enough with you to the neglect of my own realm." You do what you need to do, but don't make me come back here to whip you into shape again. Next time, Rupin won't be so nice"

Lucis motioned for the big cat to come over and give him a few kisses while he rubbed his belly. Rupin was more than happy to accommodate the request.

Lucis knew he was ill prepared for the arduous task ahead.

"I'll need weapons."

"Do I look like the Hephaestus to you?"

"A good knife or two would be welcome. I can find something to wear from whatever the monks left behind or beg something from the villagers in the next valley."

Stevyn muttered to himself, something disparaging about the deplorable lack of confidence still affecting Lucis such that he could not yet manifest his fully armed, angelic form. But he handed over two knives, one long-handled dagger, and the other a short dirk.

 "Will these do?"

"Yes, thank you."

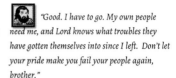 *"Good. I have to go. My own people need me, and Lord knows what troubles they have gotten themselves into since I left. Don't let your pride make you fail your people again, brother."*

Lucis hung his head in shame, even though Stevyn never bore a grudge.

"I won't. You can count on it."

 "Good. That's all I need to hear. Goodbye my friend. The ale is on you the next time we meet."

Stevyn and his supercilious cat winked out of sight, leaving Lucis with nothing besides a cold wind, the smell of a cookfire, his renewed determination to fulfill his divine mission, and … was that note? Lucis picked up the folded paper and wondered when the Knight had found the time and privacy to write him a letter. He unfolded the heavy parchment and smiled to himself as he read it.

Brother,

It has been my honor to serve you. Do not despair, even the best warriors need help sometimes. I believe you are ready to face whatever darkness comes, just believe in yourself and don't let the past effect your future. You are the best of us. Now go kick some demon ass.

Stevyn

P.S. If you fuck up again, I'll let Rupin eat you.

6 | Iron Sharpens Iron

"Buddy, I know all too well what happened to em'"- Curtis

Lucis knew what he must do. He assumed the appearance of a local peasant as he slowly made his way from village to village. As he walked through each town, he noticed that it was bereft of men. Women and children--no boys having reached adolescence--populated the small town. They looked at him as he made his way down the dusty street, their dark eyes glittering with suspicion and weariness. Their lifetime of restriction clashed with the necessity of working jobs previously held by their long-dead menfolk. These people were tired, weary beyond belief, and distrustful.

He paid them in gold and silver for their meager hospitality and what little information they could provide. He manifested the money quickly: a thought, and it was in his hand for distribution. He spent it generously, knowing that these women and children would use the coins to purchase necessities for survival.

The villagers spoke of five, well-fed foreigners who moved like predators and carried formidable weapons. They had not assaulted anyone in the village but held themselves apart and aloof. Their leader occasionally traded or paid for small items, foodstuffs, or information.

"His name was Iron," one woman volunteered.

"No, it was Smith," another woman said.

A dirty child with bare, dusty feet tugged on her sleeve and shook her head. *"No, not Iron. Forge."*

The woman's-tired eyes cleared. She smiled, exposing missing teeth.

"Yes, Forge. Hard as iron."

"He wore a red bandanna around his head," the child volunteered. *"Not like the other soldiers."*

Lucis thanked them. From there, he traced their path backward, learning little more about the elite military team who had entered those forsaken hills in pursuit of terrorists and encountered something even the worst of terrorists feared. He learned they were led by an American man, though the team was comprised of formidable, resourceful soldiers from several countries. Further discreet questioning revealed that they had emerged from the cursed cavern into which none of their own menfolk dared to venture. The team of warriors fled and waited for their leader, who trailed behind them hours later.

"He was badly wounded," a woman said, making a slashing gesture across her chest. *"Lots of blood. More soldiers came and took them away."*

Lucis speculated that they must have called for reinforcements. He asked the villagers to show him the cave. Even though the evil within had been vanquished, they remained wary. They gave him directions, unwilling to venture into the mouth of sin themselves. He understood, having touched that evil in Legion. Mere humans suffered more and healed less readily or not at all from such exposure. Still, the application of precious coin persuaded them to show him the location.

He entered the cave. The lack of light was disturbing. The townsfolk refused to go further. Once beyond the sight of any villagers, Lucis let his own aurora shine, the glow adequate for traversing the uneven, treacherous route as his senses drew him inexorably to the demon's lair.

The juxtaposition of a shaft of golden sunlight against the reeking horror spread throughout the cavern offended his senses and his sensibilities. He heard no scurry of vermin: even the rats avoided this place. A quick sideways glance, however, showed that cockroaches didn't care. They lived and endured no matter what.

Through the stink of rotted human remains, his sensitive nose caught the sour stench of fear and rage left behind by those who fought and those who succumbed. A battle occurred here, but modern weapons had not defeated the demon that had made this cavern its lair. No, modern weapons did not affect the supernatural, the occult, the extraordinary.

A glint of something pale caught his eye. Curious, Lucis walked over the grisly wreckage of a demon's feast to inspect the oddity.

The shattered blade of an ancient tomahawk still shined, though the feathers adorning the broken handle were stiff with the crusty remains of blood and gore. The blade glinted with more than steel; something else had been forged into the metal. Lucis picked up the pieces, arranging them on the flat of his palm. He sensed the history of the blade, its long line of guardians--human guardians-- who used it to defend their people. This was a weapon of righteousness.

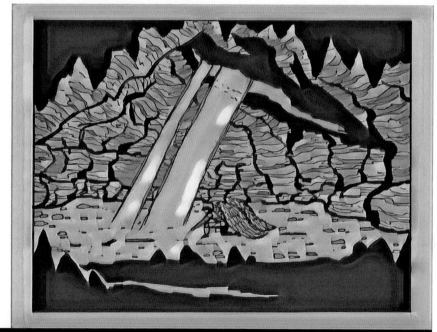

Reading the broken blade, he tried to sense the nature of the last man who had possessed it, used it. What mere man could wield such a simple weapon to defeat an ancient demon? What man would face a child of Legion with little more than an old rusted ax and the faith that it would protect him?

Obviously, not a mere man, Lucis thought, but that did not make sense.

Lucis reflected upon his own defeat, his private flight from Legion's five horrific sons. It shamed him.

Lucis gave more thought to the man who had wielded the blessed tomahawk. A man, not an angel or other holy warrior. A man, born into sin and thus in need of redemption. Salvation. He marveled at the courage that this human must have displayed, the conviction to smite evil. He admired the bravery of that man who must have known he faced something more po-tent than a mere human being. Had that man known what he wielded? Had he thought to sacrifice himself so that others might survive? The variable capacity of mankind to conduct feats of great heroism, as well as great depravity, never failed to astonish and fascinate Lucis.

The Knight exerted his will to manifest a leather pouch into which he deposited every piece of the broken tomahawk, including the crusted feathers. He prowled the vast cavern and paused now and again to pick up small bits from the floor, from the rock walls, from nooks and crannies: bullets, bits of plastic, a bent metal rod. He read the energy they held and gained a better image of the battle that left them there and the men who had waged that battle.

The spiritual energy imbued in those mementos spoke of an ancestral line of warriors, each acting from the purity of the soul, that whisper of goodness and honor cut through the miasma of evil, rage, fear, and violence like a candle's flame through the dark of night.

Reading that energy, Lucis saw the fatal blow, the blinding white light that exploded from the tomahawk as it shattered up-on the demon's body even as it slew evil. Again, the courage and faith of the man who wielded it impressed him.

Two years, he thought. It had been two years since the warrior defeated what he could not.

Lucis spent two more months tracking down the man who had wielded the blessed tomahawk. He listened to the story's villagers told him of the men who came to take away the "Demon Slayer" and his team of soldiers who fled the evil in the cave, but

they knew no more than that. With enthusiasm, they told him other stories about the newly legendary Demon Slayer, but none rang with credibility. They spoke of his kindness and generosity, how he saved this foolish boy or that beautiful maiden, made the rain quench parched fields, or drove locusts from their crops. In their tales, the Demon Slayer possessed the traits of angels and the powers of comic book superheroes. The search to find Forge began to feel like a fool's errand. Lucis needed to expand his reach. The villagers were getting him no-where, he decided to seek out hardened men; soldiers of for-tune, mercenaries, men not easily swayed by flights of fancy or folktales; men whose confidentiality could be bought for a drink or two, or perhaps a night with a loose woman. Besides Lucis could use an ale, the local fare from the villages he visited was far too spicy for his liking.

He traveled to the nearest speak-easy and set up camp disguised as a corporal in the Armed Forces of the Commonwealth. Just as Lucis suspected, the tavern was crawling with just the sort of men he was looking for. Soldiers tired from the monotony of serving their country, looking for a night of peace, or debauchery--depending on the man. After several unsuccessful attempts to obtain information relevant to his purpose, Lucis took a seat next to the man who would change his fortune.

"Get lost, pal. I ain't in the mood for conversation."

Lucis took a good look at the copper-skinned man sitting next to him and determined this was no one to be trifled with. He was tall but not lanky, with a cybernetic right arm and a patch on his left eye. Lucis peered into his soul and saw a dark, grotesque creature with needles protruding through its face and neck, staring back at him. The

sight shook Lucis to his core as he quickly released his gaze and did his best to hold it together. This man had been through something horrible, perhaps Forge had met a similar fate.

Lucis signaled to the waitress who brought a fresh bottle of gin. With a wave of his hand, he said:

 "On me."

The soldier's upper lip lifted, nodding as she poured. Lucis' keen eyes did not miss the soldier's reluctance to accept the gesture.

"Fine, you must want information. I'll answer one question but make it quick."

"What can you tell me about a man named Forge. The villagers near here say he killed a demon bat in a cave about two years ago."

"Did they now? Funny how these village folktales get started. Buy me another round, and I will tell you what I know."

Lucis nodded and signaled to the bartender to refill the man's glass. The one-eyed bronze-skinned soldier swallowed it down in one gulp.

"*I heard the stories. Like you, I took it as nonsense at first; then, I talked to a few buddies of mine who were at the scene after it all went down. From what they told me; it is hard to believe mere men could kill that many soldiers.*"

Lucis's ears perked up at the notion that Forge may not have been alone.

"So, there were five men, not just one as the villager's say?"

The man smiled and looked down at his empty glass. Lucis got the message and signaled for the waitress refill it with whatever tonic he was drinking. The soldier continued,

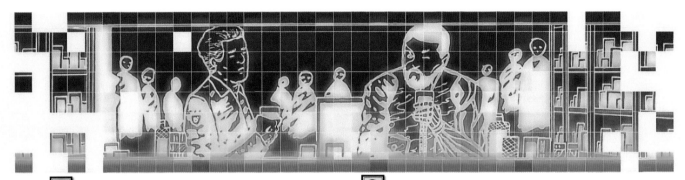

"*Not mention HOW they killed them, their bodies were melted, like goo or slime you scrape off the bottom of your shoe. Not even a flame thrower could make a mess like that.*"

"*They looked more like zombies than men. Or at least, that is what I heard. They would have no reason to lie.*"

"*No matter, they pinned the crimes on those poor bastards anyway. All five of em'*"

"*Yes and No. According to my buddies, all five went in, but only four came out on their own. They had to drag that last guy out of there, kicking and screaming.*"

"*Going on about a demon and whatnot. I am sure that is how these tales get started.*"

The soldier paused, guzzled his gin concoction, and continued,

"Do tell."

 "Again, who is to say. The military police arrived hours after reinforcements showed up. I don't' blame them for locking them up. Poor bastards."

"Hellgate is what happened to them. They sent those sons of bitches to Hellgate. I bet my good eye on that one."

"I mean, someone had to take the fall for the death of five hundred soldiers, and it damn sure was not going to be a demon bat that no one has ever seen."

"What is Hellgate?"

"How daft are you?"

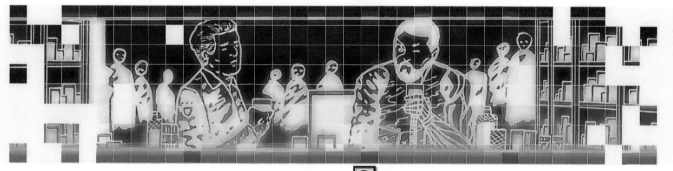

Intrigued, Lucis pressed further.

"Do you know what happened to the war criminals, Forge in particular."

The one-eyed soldier took a long pause staring down into his cup. He breathed in deep and replied

 "Buddy, I know all too well what happened to em."

 "Every mercenary or trooper worth a damn knows the myth of Hellgate. Well, buddy, I can tell you, it ain't no myth, that place is real."

Lucis smiled and placed a hundred-dollar bill in front of the soldier,

"Indulge me."

 "Fine, it's your money."

"Hellgate is the place they send war criminals or anyone the Commonwealth wants to get rid of. A place off the books so the Alliance can maintain their squeaky-clean image".

 "Sons of bitches. We do all their dirty work, and the minute we violate their so-called moral code..."

"So, you have been there?"

 "Look at you, with your perfectly pressed uniform. You are fresh out of boot camp, aren't you corporal?"

 "Probably some rich kid who just graduated college looking for an opportunity to boss some grunts around."

 "Well, I am from a different stock—a real soldier. Sixteen combat missions, over two hundred confirmed kills."

The soldier replied in anger,

 "Yes, I have been there. Does that bother you? Are you my judge now?"

"No, I did not mean it like that."

 "Could have fooled me, boy scout."

 "Hell, for what I did for this nation, I should have received a medal, but they handed me over to the German instead. Sure, I tortured and maimed a few innocents in the name of the Commonwealth, but I did what needed to be done."

 "Could you do the same, boy?"

"No,"

Lucis said as he hung his head, playing along. A Knight of his caliber knew all too well the hard choices made in the name of justice.

"Damn right. Only a few of us have the guts to do what is needed to protect the freedoms these civilians enjoy. I am proud of what I did and would do it again if called upon."

His eyes told a different story, one of regret and dismay, but he continued anyway

 " I spent forty days in that place. I was just released a few months ago. Now I spend my nights here, trying to forget"

 "As for those poor bastards, I only know stories, whispers from cellmates during my time there."

 "The rumor was there were five soldiers, more mercenaries really who had withstood the German's torture methods for over two years."

 "A feat never accomplished before according to most."

"Who is the German?"

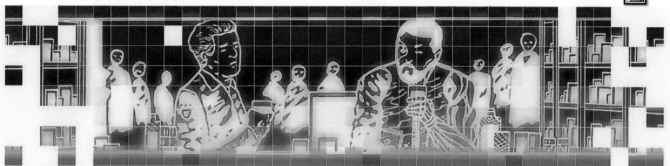

Lucis placed another hundred-dollar bill on the table and said,

"So what of Forge? What do you know about the five men?"

 "Right," the soldier took a moment to collect himself.

 "Forgive me for rambling on about my plight, you are a man of purpose, I can see that."

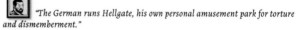 *"Not too bright, are you?"*

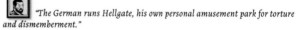 *"The German runs Hellgate, his own personal amusement park for torture and dismemberment."*

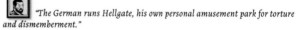 *"I was there for forty days, and I confessed to my crimes, seven hundred and thirty days is another matter altogether."*

"*Their ability to withstand torture is legend amongst the damned souls that occupy that accursed place. The one thing that gives them all hope. It is understood that those five have endured all sorts of torture, chemical cocktails, extreme heat and cold, electric shock, sensory deprivation, waterboarding, poisonous spiders, you name it, they have endured it. But no one knows why they choose to suffer and not just confess.*"

 "*Personally, I think it was to send a message to the powers that be at the Commonwealth that they cannot be controlled. Sort of a big fuck you to them and the German. They definitely had my support. Bad-assess, every one of em'*"

Lucis decided to inject a few kind words, it could not hurt in helping him get the rest of the information he needed

"*Well, you do not seem like a pushover by any account. I am sure you gave the German fits as well.*"

The soldier smiled at that remark.

 "*Damn right. I even spit in that smug son of a bitch's face when he removed my eye from the socket. I would not give him the satisfaction of even a whimper when the cornea dangled on my cheek, but even I have my limits, and the creature was too much for me.*"

"*The creature?*"

 "*You heard me.*"

"A creature from another world, a dark world, lurks the halls of Hellgate, tormenting victims at will. Rumor has it that it is the German's pet, his secret weapon to get his subject to crack, or kill themselves for that matter. I didn't believe in such nonsense until it came to visit me that night, crawling above my bed on six legs like a spider. A grotesque, gnarled, twisted creature, with thick iron stakes impaled into its body, whip marks across its chest and back-- the beast got inside my brain. It tormented me relentlessly, making me relive the horrible acts I committed on those innocent little kids over and over. Every time I clipped a finger or cut off a toe, I could feel their terrible anguish but amplified a thousand times more. Over and over, all night long. The next morning, I confessed to my crimes and was transferred out of there to a proper military prison--But to this day, I can still feel its presence inside my soul, mocking me, tormenting me, no end in sight."

"I drink to drown it out, but even that is starting to wear off."

 "I picked up a drill once determined to drive out the thoughts buried in my head. The prison guard stopped me before I could go through with it."

The soldier lifted his glass and drunk deep,

"Almost, my friend. Just one more question. Where can I find this Hellgate and this German you speak of?"

That comment brought a rare smile to the soldier's face.

 "Man, you really are a noob, aren't you? You don't find Hellgate, that kind of place finds you."

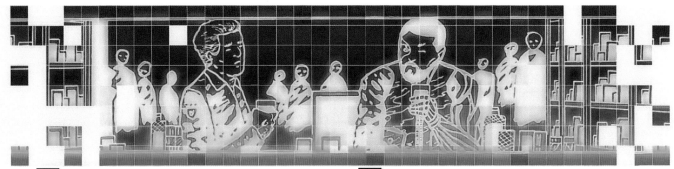

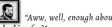 *"Aww, well, enough about that. Did you get the information you were looking for?"*

Lucis pondered on the question as he tried to recall his own vision in his head when he first glared into the soul of the burly man before him. Could the being he spoke of be the same one he saw, or was it a creature at all? Perhaps something more sinister and evil was at work here; could it be a child of Legion lurked the halls of Hellgate? His daydream was cut short by his companion.

 "Well, are we finished now?"

 "I have no idea where to even begin to look. If I had to guess, it would be somewhere underground beneath a mountain or waterfall or something, well hidden so that no one could find it."

 "I was bound and gagged my whole journey to that dreadful place, the standard protocol for those wanting to cover up the Commonwealth's misdeeds"

 "No one could find that place, friend. Not in a million years."

"One last thing. Will you allow me to pray for you? Perhaps I can help to remove the horrible visions you see at night?"

The soldier burst into laughter

 "Ooh, mister, that is a good one. Don't you know a cursed man when you see one?"

"Can at least call on you again sometime? I might have more questions."

 "Sure thing, The name's Curtis, Curtis Johnson."

 "I live in a small house two blocks from here, you can't miss it. You bring the gin, and I'll answer any damn question you want."

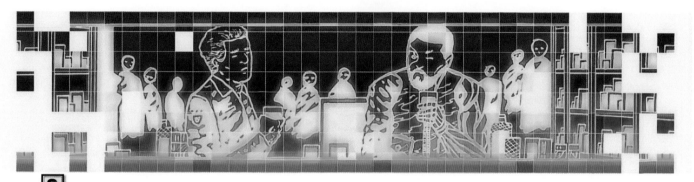

 "I deserve to be punished for my sins, and no pencil neck goody-two-shoes is going to change that."

 "Leave me be"

A single tear fell from the soldier's good eye.

 "We are done here."

Lucis nodded and shook his hand,

"Corporal Smith, Wayne Smith."

Lucis hung his head and sighed. *If he only knew...* he thought to himself. One-touch and the soldier could have received the spiritual healing he so desperately desired, just the one small gesture to change the course of his life forever. But humans have free will, and even a warrior, such a Lucis, could not interfere with man's wishes.

He could feel the sorrow in his soul; the man wanted to change. He just lacked the courage to forgive--himself. A condition Lucis knew all too well in mankind.

The Angel of Light thanked the man one last time and left the bar with more questions than he had when he went in.

Was Forge one of the five men at Hellgate, the soldier, spoke of? Had Forge confessed and been released? Who was the mysterious creature, and did it also torment Forge and his cohorts? The most pressing of his concerns was how in the hell was he ever going to find this mysterious man who could potentially be the key to stopping Legion's children from infiltrating the spirits of man and terrorizing the Earth.

Lucis needed to rest and ponder on the things he learned; a clean refresh of his spirit would do him good. Try as he might, he still had not regained all of his former strength since his battle with Legion. Stevyn did what he could, but wounds from such an adversary take time to heal fully, especially on the in-side.

He awoke from his slumber to the incessant chirping of birds and bright glare of the sun. Three days had passed since he decided to rest his bones and revamp his soul for the journey ahead—an average amount of rest for angel such as himself perhaps a bit more for good measure.

Feeling refreshed, Lucis decided to give Mr. Johnson a visit before heading off. He figured he would give the poor soul one more chance at redemption if only he would take it.

Lucis needed to rest and ponder on the things he learned; a clean refresh of his spirit would do him good. Try as he might, he still had not regained all of his former strength since his battle with Legion. Stevyn did what he could, but wounds from such an adversary take time to heal fully, especially on the in-side.

He awoke from his slumber to the incessant chirping of birds and bright glare of the sun. Three days had passed since he decided to rest his bones and revamp his soul for the journey ahead—an average amount of rest for angel such as himself perhaps a bit more for good measure.

Feeling refreshed, Lucis decided to give Mr. Johnson a visit before heading off. He figured he would give the poor soul one more chance at redemption if only he would take it.

A few blocks from the tavern, he noticed a quaint house with a blue roof, a considerable change from the other brown roof huts in the same vicinity.

Can't miss it, just as he said... Lucis thought to himself as he approached the residence. Stepping foot upon the property, he felt the eerie silence. Although birds sang and insects buzzed, and somewhere in the distance a cow mooed, the house and its grounds were filled with an uncanny lack of sound. Suspecting the worst, he knocked on the door. The sound echoed inside the house, and the door remained shut. He put his hand on the doorknob, and it turned, offering no resistance. His foreboding grew as he stepped inside the cool interior. His keen ears caught the telltale buzzing of flies. An all too familiar stench assaulted his nose.

Lucis sighed, knowing the worst and needing to confirm it with his own eyes. He prowled through the house and found the soldier dangling from a rope slung over an exposed rafter in the attic. He wondered if he should have offered more than a peaceful place to rest where a man could dwell upon his thoughts. That man's thoughts and memories had killed him, the weight of his sins breaking his neck as surely as the noose from which he hung.

He wondered: Did Curtis expect too much from himself, surely Lucis nor the Everlasting did not. Despair was a cardinal sin, yet he knew that a broken soul needed succor and forgiveness rather than eternal damnation. He murmured a quick prayer his soul; it mattered not. His eternal destination was already sealed, the penalty for taking one's life was clear and irreversible, even for a Knight of the Trinity.

Leaving the house, Lucis felt urgency press upon him. He needed to find Forge and fast; before his soul succumbed to the same fate--but where to start?

Lucis had no idea where to begin his search, but that did not deter him. He would search the world over if necessary, but first, he vowed that no one would hear about Curtis's shame. That was the least he could do for the unfortunate soul. The pupils of his eyes flared. In an instant, flames engulfed the dwelling, a raging fire, bent on destruction. As Lucis flew away, he watched without expression as the house burned to the ground.

 *For Curtis Jackson*...the warrior knight exclaimed.

Lucis smiled as his search for Forge the demon slayer began anew.

7 | Light's Quest

"Angels are real"- Bystander

His light has faded, Lucis murmured to himself as he reached out with all his otherworldly senses to find the soldier whose courage and integrity inspired him. The spark of goodness and pure light in Forge Qualateqa's soul had vanished.

Lucis knew only one of two things had happened: Forge had died and was beyond the realms of man, or the weight of the world and years of torture had turned Forge into someone else, someone beyond his aid. Given what the soldier had endured, Lucis could understand the latter, although he would never condone such a thing. Humans were all too eager to blame God for their misfortunes instead thanking him for their many trials and tribulations. *Without tests, how could one get stronger? Iron sharpens iron,* Lucis pondered. The human condition always puzzled Lucis, so much power, yet so little faith. The angel shook his head to clear his mind of speculation. Speculation would get him nowhere: he had one man to find among billions. With dedicated single-mindedness, Lucis dedicated himself to tracking down the man who slew a demon. Distance and time presented no obstacle. His search first took him to one of the many war-torn countries in Africa, where people lived within a constant flux of changing regimes. In those dangerous areas, one man's freedom fighter also served as another man's terrorist.

Lucis recognized that women on either side fared poorly. However, something may have brought Forge Qaletaga to this tropical place, where humans preferred the lesser danger of large predators in the jungle than the usually violent consequences of meeting their kind.

The air hung heavily with humidity, and one practically needed gills to breathe. Trekking through the hot, humid misery of the African jungle, Lucis entered a village in chaos. He maintained discretion through invisibility, eavesdropping on the villagers, hoping to catch a whisper of the name of the man he knew. Instead of whispers, he heard the cries and laments of the people about a band of soldiers pillaging their village and taking their children as hostages. Any attempt to fight back came with a grave consequence. Those who were left wailed and wept as they dug graves and mourned for the dead and the missing.

Lucis thought to himself: *Was this the group of soldiers he was looking for? Could Forge have stooped so low as to become a mercenary and kidnap innocent children?* He quickly dismissed the thought as fast as it occurred.

Whoever committed such atrocities was evil, and he resolved to deal with that evil swiftly and without remorse.

Filled with righteous anger and the burning desire to see justice done, Lucis went after them. He found the children clustered into a frightened group, desperate for the hope of rescue. Cloaking himself from human senses, he infiltrated the soldiers' encampment to learn their intent.

The soldier was Darfur, a murderous group of rebels whose lust for power in Central Africa was well known. Among murder, espionage, and kidnapping, they were also known for cannibalism. Lucis had learned that the soldiers intended to indoctrinate the boys and prostitute the girls. Lucis' stomach churned as he learned their fate. He knew he must act fast to save the children; after all, the angel was the sworn protector of the realm, and, if the warrior could not protect

innocent children, then what good was he? The quest for Forge would have to wait. Lucis had other business to attend.

He raced first to answer the screams of a girl who squirmed and struggled beneath an adult man who pinned her to the ground. A yelp of pain followed the crack of an open-handed slap. Lucis, still under the cloak of invisibility, drew his mighty sword and swung. The keen edge of the shining blade cleaved through mortal flesh like the clichéd hot knife through butter and stopped a scant finger's breadth from the girl's own body. She screamed again as her rapist's head dropped with a sickening thud and rolled aside. Blood gushed like a macabre fountain from the dead man's neck even as the body collapsed on top of the girl. Lucis kicked the body off the child to allow her the opportunity to stand and run.

WITH DEADLY INTENT, HE SNEAKED THROUGH THE ENCAMPMENT, JUDGING EVERY SOLDIER IN HIS PATH. FLASHES OF LIGHT EMANATING FROM LUCIS' SWORD ALERTED HIS VICTIMS TOO LATE. BY THE TIME A SOLDIER FIXED HIS GAZE, THE KEEN EDGE HAD BITTEN INTO HIS FLESH, A FATAL STROKE EACH TIME. THEY PANICKED AS THEIR BRETHREN FELL, ONE BY ONE, TO THAT MYSTERIOUS LIGHT.

Some soldiers started shooting in circles. Others stabbed the air around them with their hunting knives. None of it mattered as they were cut down swiftly at the amazement and astonishment of the children in bondage.

After slaughtering the battalion like so much vermin, the warrior angel called out to the frightened children,

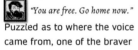 *"You are free. Go home now."* Puzzled as to where the voice came from, one of the braver children cried out, *"We don't know the way."*

A light appeared before the traumatized children gathered amid the stench of blood and gore and violence. Its silvery glow beckoned to them.

"Follow me. I shall lead you home. If anyone asks you what happened, you say God saved you because you were pure of light."

One child struck up a folk song from their village. The others soon joined in. It gave them courage and hope and spoke of their immense gratitude to what had occurred. The children followed the floating wisp of light, which winked out moments before they entered the outskirts of their village.

Grieving adults turned and watched open-mouthed in astonishment as the children marched back home, hymns of praise pouring from their throats. They rushed forward to embrace their children and offer comfort to those now orphaned. In the manner of their people, relatives, and close family friends offered to foster the orphans. When one of the mothers asked her son what had happened and how they were able to make it back home, the boy replied,

"God saved us because our souls are pure."

The search followed the trajectory of Forge's travels, for the man left a strong impression upon the people he met--well, those who lived after meeting him. The soldier lived by the sword, which conferred upon him a life of continuing violence as he hired that sword to any who paid the exorbitant fee his skill and experience demanded. The angel follows rumors and whispers across the vast ocean to another continent.

Lucis found himself in another jungle, just as hot, sticky, and miserable as the one in Africa. Surely someone in India must have heard of the whereabouts of such an extraordinary man? There was only one way to find out. Cries of terror and pain drew his attention in the ordinarily quiet jungle. He raced toward the noise and came upon a man doing his best to shield a child from a tiger. The orange and black striped beast had blood smeared on his white muzzle, which drew Lucis' gaze to the man's ruined leg.

The man wielded a large stick in his hand, which he used to fend off the angry cat. The Bengal tiger crouched, growling in defense of its territory. Lucis knew no evil spirit possessed the beast; it exhibited only a natural reaction to having been startled. The tiger was young and, likely, hungry. He shook his head at the foolishness of man to have wandered into a tiger's domain. However, the child earned no blame for the man's stupidity and did not deserve to suffer for it.

The tiger sprang forward as the man covered the child with his body and swung the stick. The stick connected with a meaty thwack; the young beast recoiled in pain. Enraged, it leaped again. Calling upon his sparring with Stevyn and Rupin, Lucis sheathed his sword, cloaked himself in invisibility, and jumped into the fray to grapple with the tiger.

THE MAN STOOD IN SHOCK AS SOMEONE OR SOMETHING KNOCKED THE TIGER OFF ITS FEET. HE HEARD THE ROAR AND THE GRUNTS, THE EERIE SOUND OF CLAWS SCRAPING AGAINST SOMETHING METALLIC. HE DID NOT KNOW WHETHER THE TIGER COULD SEE WHAT IT FOUGHT, BUT FIGHT IT DID, FIRST WITH RAGE AND THEN WITH GROWING DESPERATION. THE MAN CLOSED HIS EYES IN TERROR AS HE SHIELDED THE TODDLER AND CHANTED PRAYERS FOR DELIVERANCE, PROMISING TO REFORM THEIR WAYS AND DEDICATE THEMSELVES TO SERVING OTHERS IF THEY SURVIVED. WHEN THE HORRIBLE NOISES STOPPED, HE OPENED HIS EYES.

The man yelped in horror and scrambled back from the unseeing eyes of the dead tiger's head beside them. The man drew his knife with the intent of stabbing the beast, punishment forever messing with the likes of man. *"Don't,"* a deep voice intoned. It filled the area, silencing noisy birds and even buzzing insects.

The man looked around but saw no one who spoke. He immediately dropped to his knees and lowered his head in deference to a higher power.

"Go home and don't return to this part of the jungle. Tell your people to stay out and let the animals have this domain," the voice ordered.

The two scrambled to their feet and fled, the elder using the stick for support. When they were out of sight, Lucis materialized and squatted next to the tiger's carcass. He ran his mailed hand through the thick fur and bowed his head in regret for having killed the animal. He thought to himself, Rupin would be upset with me for killing his kin.

Lucis' hunt crossed over many lands, going from one exotic culture to another. One of those cultures survived despite the oppressive regime that systematically stifled market competition and squashed human rights. The angel rather enjoyed the ancient culture's enduring strength, formalized beauty, and ritual etiquette. He knew it wasn't perfect, but he also knew that pleasure, beauty, and appreciation did not require perfection. Still, China held high economic and political power on the planet that even an emissary of God needed to treat with respect, especially in Beijing.

The government square was in an uproar. Rioting erupted in the streets as parades of irate citizens marched, chanting protests government oppression and corruption. The shatter of glass preceded the whump of firebombs exploding as rioters threw them through the windows of government buildings and the homes of government officials. Shouts and screams of rage and pain mingled with the shriek of sirens and the blare of loudspeakers demanding that citizens stand down. Hidden from the sight of man--although a few stray cats looked his way, because one couldn't fool them--Lucis smiled to himself. He rather liked seeing such a spirit of courage in people. It was rare to see such defiance in an age of self-indulgence and indifference.

The roar of industrial-sized engines overwhelmed the general cacophony.

People's voices quieted as they turned to face this new threat: tanks. The massive treads of the tanks crunched over pavement and anything else in their path. Lucis frowned, appalled that the government would turn its military personnel and weapons against its citizens. He watched in admiration as people lined up in front of the approaching tanks, linking arms in defiant solidarity. The large vehicles rumbled forward. The loudspeakers blared again with a new message: *"Disperse or die."*

Lucis witnessed fear and determination on the faces of a culture he'd long admired, a people of whom he was fond. The tanks slowed but continued their approach down the city street. Drones, media personnel, and ordinary people with cell phones recorded the imminent clash and impending horror.

"No," he muttered under his breath.

 "No, I will not allow this injustice."

FILLED WITH RIGHTEOUS FURY, HE LAUNCHED HIMSELF AT THE LEAD VEHICLE. SPECTATORS GASPED IN AWE AS THE TANK SUDDENLY FLIPPED AS THOUGH SLAMMING INTO A WALL AND TIPPING UPSIDE DOWN, TREADS RUNNING LIKE AN OVERTURNED BEETLE'S LEGS MIGHT CHURN. UNABLE TO AVOID THE SUDDEN AND UNEXPECTED UPSET, TWO TANKS RAN OVER THE ONE WHO HAD SOMERSAULTED AND LANDED UPSIDE DOWN. THE TWO VEHICLES CRASHED INTO IT, KILLING THE SOLDIERS TRAPPED INSIDE.

Cheers erupted from the populace. Someone, infused with an extra helping of defiance against an agnostic government, shouted,

"It's a miracle! It's a miracle! Praise GOD!"

Falling to their knees, others took up the chant, thumbing their noses further at a government that tried to deny its people religious faith.

Lucis tracked Forge to the City of Light: Paris. A famous political upstart whose influence exceeded another powerful politician's tolerance had died under suspicious circumstances. As much as Lucis did not want to accept that Forge could have orchestrated the alleged accident, he had to admit that it was plausible. Whispered rumors of the mercenary soldier's brutality and lack of remorse indeed testified to that possibility. However, he hit another dead end and needed a moment to mull over the information. The heady scent of coffee caught his attention, and he decided to stop at a local café. Assuming a guise as one of the many Middle Eastern immigrants in the city, he entered the locale, purchased a cup of Turkish coffee,

and took a seat. A small group of men in traditional Middle Eastern garb conversed in low tones, their words filled with hatred and spite. Either they did not know the customer sitting near them could overhear them, or they did not care.

As he sipped at the genuinely excellent brew--really, no one made coffee (or croissants) quite as well as the French--he eavesdropped on the conversation at the table behind him. His concern grew, and righteous anger began to simmer. Once again, he decided to pause his search for Forge in favor of upholding justice and protecting the people he loved.

He listened to their plot to destroy the Eiffel Tower with a supreme lack of care for the innocent people who would be killed. He finished his coffee and rose from the table. Walking away, he kept his ears attuned to their conversation as he rounded a corner and faded from human sight. He crept back and stood over them, his eavesdropping blatant even if they could not see, smell, or hear him.

Lucis bided his time. Perched unseen in the large iron structure, he watched as terrorists planted a bomb and heard the words *"mercury switch."*

Moving the weapon once it was activated was not an option. Any movement would cause the mercury to slide and trigger the explosion. When the terrorists left, Lucis made his way over to it. He projected a miasma of unwelcome. People in the area shuddered and walked away, never knowing why they obeyed a strange urge to go elsewhere when he'd cleared a sizeable space, Lucis dove at the bomb, dislodging it and curling his armored body around it. The shift in position detonated the explosive. Lucis's ears rang with the sound of the explosion. He felt the punch of the blast, forcibly contained by his body. He grunted aloud, the loud noise drawing attention from people standing a safe distance away. They saw the spurt of orange flame, the black billow of smoke. They gaped in awe, many holding up their cell phones to record the event.

"A bomb detonated at the Eiffel Tower," a quick-thinking journalist reported, holding up his cell phone.

"But, somehow, something contained the explosion which would have toppled the iconic structure. We don't know why or how the bomb failed in its task, but all of Paris is grateful. We can only assume a higher power is at work here. We can only assume that Parisians and tourists have witnessed a genuine miracle! God must be real!"

Lucis crossed the Atlantic Ocean to the United States of America, where he felt sure he could pick up new leads for his search.

What better place to start than New York City? And why not indulge in a coffee at a sidewalk café, too? He hoped that the Italian pastry shop was still in business. Assuming the guise of a Greenwich Village hipster, he purchased a large cappuccino and a cannoli and took a seat to enjoy a bit of lazy sunshine and people watching while he plotted out his next steps. Hearing nothing but the usual inconsequential conversation around him, he sipped at the coffee and picked up the day's newspaper left behind by another patron. Scanning the articles, he read about the growing conflict over the new border between the Commonwealth and Mexico, with the latter country's ambitious goal to build the most technologically advanced border wall ever constructed. Running straight across northern Mexico from the eastern part of the Rio Grande to the western coast, the Commonwealth stole hundreds of square miles of territory from its disgruntled southern neighbor. However, the article mentioned nothing about that.

Pictures of the president surrounded by his protective detail accompanied the article. The garish media affair showed the self-important president looking skyward with a pious expression and a familiar figure standing guard in the background next to the first lady and their two children.

CommonWealth Gazzette

ENGLISH EDITION

AT LAST!

PRESIDENT PLANS TO ATTEND UNVEILING CEREMONY FOR COMPLETION OF BORDER WALL

CommonWealth President Jonathan R. Rothchild announced his participation in the unveiling ceremony for Project Pegasus, the largest border protection project in history. Sources confirm that he will deliver a speech to commemorate the event.

President giving a speech at the wall groundbreaking ceremony

The president called the construction "a crowning achievement of his service to the country." President Rothchild also praised construction crews and security forces for their part in securing the country's border despite four years of political opposition, defunding efforts, and violent attacks upon the project and construction workers.

In closing, the president encouraged all his supporters to come out and participate in what he called "a monumental event in CommonWealth history."

Lucis gasped. All that travel... all that searching... all that effort expended. In the end, all he needed to do was pick up a newspaper. The tortured man he saw matched the descriptions related by the villagers and the gaunt, unbroken warrior he remembered from the facility where Forge had been interrogated. A red bandana held back the man's long hair, the ends shown fluttering in a hot breeze. The high, sharp cheekbones and coppery skin proclaimed his Native American heritage.

The angel breathed a sigh of relief at the knowledge that the soldier had not died, nor killed himself. No, this man had given himself to more turbulence and strife. In the newspaper photo, Lucis could see violence surrounding the former soldier like a cloud.

Lucis hoped he could lead Forge Qaletaga back to the light.

The angel set down the cup and the newspaper and left, fading from sight as he rounded a corner.

The green gleam of the Statue of Liberty hailed him as he streamed westward. As he adjusted his trajectory, he angled over downtown New York, sailing over the many skyscrapers.

BOOM!

THE SOUND WAS SUPERSONIC.

PAIN EXPLODED THROUGHOUT LUCIS'S CORE, THEN RADIATED OUTWARD UNTIL EVEN HIS FINGERS, TOES, AND THE ENDS OF HIS HAIR HURT. HE HURTLED TO THE GROUND, CRASHING INTO THE CONCRETE. THE CRATER DESTABILIZED THE TOWER NEXT TO HIM, CAUSING IT TO COLLAPSE IN A

HUMONGOUS CLOUD OF CHOKING DUST AND RUBBLE AND STIFLED SCREAMS. THE STENCH OF BLOOD AND DEATH AND TERROR ASSAULTED HIS NOSE AS MASONRY BLOCKS CRASHED DOWN UPON HIM.

Sickened and furious by what had happened and his failure to prevent it, Lucis powered through the heap of the demolished building and broken humans that lay scattered among the ruin like so many rag dolls. But bloody. So bloody. Bursting from the destruction, he looked around, wondering if the military were testing weapons and shot him from the sky, even though none of their technology should have been able to detect his presence.

After a long moment of disorientation and fury that morphed into a keen desire for vengeance against whoever shot him down, he realized that bystanders... SAW HIM.

No one on Earth had ever SAW HIM before, towering above all armor glistening in the moonlight. It was forbidden to reveal your pure form to man, by the rules of the Order. Lucis was always so careful to mask himself as some beggar, buffoon, or vagabond, not worth or remembrance. They pointed and shouted, some epithets, some cries of praise, some merely wailing for their lost loved ones. Some voices accused him of killing people and destroying property in some sickening publicity stunt. Many held up their cell phones to take pictures and record the magnificent, armored being whose pristine white wings flapped slowly as he hovered above the enormous pile of rubble and death.

With the extrasensory perception of his kind, Lucis felt the imminent arrival of conflict. He knew he would meet whoever had knocked him from the sky,

heedless of the collateral damage that resulted.

Some sense had him whirling about to face an opponent where none had existed a second before. It was humanoid with three arms, sufficiently as large as an average adult man. It crawled down a nearby tower. Glowing blue, the alien creature leaped at Lucis, a blade of light extending from its closed fist. Lucis engaged. The creature's swordsmanship impressed the angel, but Lucis was not known among his brethren for sloppy fighting skills. The laser blade of the creature's sword clashed with Lucis' own holy weapon, a strange clang that reverberated among the tall buildings. Their battle pushed them to the ground where humans scurried back and shouted encouragement as they dodged parked vehicles, potholes, broken concrete, and other debris.

"What are you?"

Lucis snarled as he parried an attack and struck again. The alien's lips peeled back to reveal serrated teeth, sharp and deadly in a reptilian face. It lunged at him. Lucis wasted no further time or effort on the creature: his holy blade sliced through the alien's arm wielding the laser sword, cauterizing the wound as the limb fell to the ground, still clutching the weapon.

The alien screamed with pain and rage, then bowed its head and begged for mercy. Lucis, who had not thought of humanity toward this creature, stayed his hand because the creature spoke in a human tongue.

"Spare me, Lucis,"

the creature said and held up its remaining two hands, palms open and facing outward.

"I am but a messenger."

"Messengers don't normally attack those to whom they deliver the messages--And how in the hell do you know my name?"

The creature shuddered in fear, stuttering as he spoke:

"K-K-Killing you was the message "Y-Y-You must leave Earth and never return."

"This is my realm, alien! Why should I leave?"

"Your miraculous acts inspire hope. Since the defeat of Fear, my master cannot and will not tolerate this resurgence of hope among humankind"

Lucis paused to wonder who the mysterious being's master might be. Perhaps Legion, he reasoned, except that Legion was dead and his sons set free.

The short time he used to consider the alien's word and meaning gave it enough opportunity to regenerate the lost third arm. It placed all three hands upon its head. The action caused a vibration that echoed in waves of vertigo. Lucis fought to retain his senses even as humans below dropped to their knees, clutching at their own heads and wailing in pain.

More shouts and screams floated upon currents of air as the alien's form swelled and blurred. It grunted and groaned, caustic spittle dribbling from its mouth. With a final grunt, the alien split into three separate beings, the fission emitting an obscene, wet, sucking noise.

Lucis blinked, thinking that vertigo affected him more intensely than he thought. That thought vanished when all three of the beings attacked him with teeth and claws. The cunning and coordinated attack took him by

surprise, and he swiftly realized that he could not fight off all three attackers at once.

LUCIS SHOT UPWARD, HOPING TO ESCAPE THE ASSASSINS. HOWEVER, THEIR POWERFUL HAUNCHES PROPELLED THEM UPWARD IN MIGHTY LEAPS THAT HAD THEM CLINGING TO HIM. THEY BIT AND CLAWED AT THE ANGEL'S ARMOR TO MAINTAIN THEIR HOLD UPON HIM, ONE CLIMBING HIS BODY TO SINK ITS SERRATED TEETH INTO HIS NECK DESPITE A MOUTHFUL OF ENCHANTED METAL.

HOWLING IN AGONY, LUCIS FLEW HIGHER AND HIGHER. HIS WINGS STRAINED AGAINST THE ADDED WEIGHT THEY WERE NEVER MEANT TO SUPPORT. AS THE ALIEN CHOMPED DOWN AGAIN AND LUCIS FELT BLOOD RUNNING DOWN HIS SKIN, HE KNEW HE HAD TO DO SOMETHING FAST. OR DIE.

SWIVELING IN MID-AIR, HE DOVE LIKE A FALCON TOWARD THE GROUND, TWISTING AND TURNING IN A TIGHT SPIRAL DESIGNED TO MAKE HIS ATTACKERS DIZZY. THE ALIENS CLUTCHED AT HIM AS THEIR RIDE HEADED STRAIGHT FOR THE PAVEMENT BELOW.

CHUNKS OF ASPHALT EXPLODED INTO THE AIR AS THE ANGEL DRILLED DOWNWARD. THE ALIENS JUMPED OFF HIM THE INSTANT BEFORE HE CRASHED INTO THE EON. THE THREE ALIEN SOLDIERS PEERED OVER THE EDGE OF THE DEEP, DEEP CRATER WHERE THE SILVERY ARMORED ANGEL HAD DISAPPEARED BEYOND SIGHT AND LAUGHED.

Around them, the crowd grew silent in awe and horror. The aliens turned to face the onlookers and removed their heavy helmets to reveal reptilian faces. Displaying fearsome teeth, they hissed at the puny humans. One intrepid reporter approached

holding a microphone, which he extended to the closest alien. Before the man could say a word, the creature snatched the microphone from the man's hand and, with another hand, drove a claw through the reporter's skull. The reporter's expression froze in a feeling of horrified surprise even as the body sagged and crumpled to the ground. Gasps of horror reverberated through the onlookers.

The alien looked at the microphone, then tossed it aside. Opening its mouth, it spoke, the guttural pronunciation carrying easily throughout the city:

"We are Trarkad. Your champion has been defeated by our superior technology and intelligence. All will fall to our glorious might. You will all be witnesses to ascension on this pitiful planet. We will feast on your flesh and--"

Before the alien could pontificate further, a bright white light exploded from the hole. The Trarkad aliens turned to face it and gaped in astonishment. Magnificent in his full glory, Lucis hovered above them, a sword is drawn, glorious light emanated from his body.

Before the alien could pontificate further, a bright white light exploded from the hole. The Trarkad aliens turned to face it and gaped in astonishment. Magnificent in his full glory, Lucis hovered above them, a sword is drawn, glorious light emanated from his body.

Lucis took advantage of the aliens' moment of stunned astonishment to lop off the heads of two of them in one mighty blow. The edge of his holy sword cut through their armor and flesh with ease. Green ichor splattered rubble, bricks, and nearby vehicles, eating through the materials like acid. The

remaining alien leaped to evade the next strike, but Lucis shot forth and ensnared the Trarkad around the neck with one gauntleted hand. The alien hissed and squirmed but could not break free of the angel's hold as they rose into the air. It begged for mercy, but Lucis did not fall for the same ruse twice.

The Seventh Spark – Knights of the Trinity

The angel chanted the oath of his guild as he squeezed

WE ARE KNIGHTS
OF THE TRINITY
WARRIORS OF THE
ALMIGHTY GOD
DEFENDERS OF
TRUTH
PROTECTORS OF
THE WEAK
GUARDIANS OF THE
TWELVE REALMS OF
MEN.
WE PLEDGE OUR
SPIRITS, OUR
SWORDS, AND OUR
SHIELDS IN
SERVICE,
FOR GLORY, PRIDE,
AND HONOR.
MAY ALL FORCES
OF EVIL DIE AT OUR
HANDS!
FOR THE NAME OF
THE LORD SHALL
FOREVER BE
PRAISED,
NOW AND FOREVER.
AMEN!

The bones in the alien's neck succumbed to the pressure of his grip, flesh oozing through mailed fingers like so much green slime. He opened his hand to drop the dead alien, then lashed out with his sword on the other side to sever the body in half. Slimy green ichor splattered when the pieces hit the ground. People who did not dodge the droplets quickly enough cried out in pain as their flesh burned.

Lucis thought quickly. There were so many questions that required answers. As far as he knew, alien life was nonexistent on this planet or any other worlds according to his cohorts. Why now, why here, and how did they know I existed, he thought to himself...too many questions, too many questions. The one thing he did know is that he needed to remove all the evidence he could of these life forms. His curiosity fails in comparison to his human

counterparts. Lucis knew the military scientists were on their way, ready to dissect and exploit their new find. He could not let that happen. He now knew what he must do.

Lucis swooped down to collect the bodies of the fallen Trarkad soldiers. With another burst of light, he flew away, leaving behind the devastation of a ruined city block where a small but significant battle in the eternal war occurred.

The airwaves and the internet exploded with eyewitness accounts and media reports of the strange happenings that left no physical trace of the angel, the aliens, the laser swords: only dead bodies, destroyed property, and deep, deep holes in the ground. But those eyewitnesses spoke of what they saw: a miracle. In an interview, one child summed up the experience:

Angels are real.

8 | Garden of the Damned

EPISODE EIGHT
- Lucis seeks out Michael to make sense of his findings in New York

"All things are possible"- Michael

Archangel! Lucis approached Michael, went to one knee, and laid body parts of the rotting alien species at his feet.

"Look at what I found on Earth, I..."

Michael back turned to Lucis, held up his hand signaling now was not the time for hysterics, but time for peace and reflection.

He paid no mind to Lucis's theatrics and continued sprucing one of the many trees in his garden.

Lucis had never been to Michaels's garden before, although he had heard stories of its magnificence and beauty. He breathed in deep and took a moment to take it all in. The sight brought him to tears. The enormous valley stretched beyond his view. Lush greenery, flowers of every color of the rainbow, and trees bearing every sort of fruit enveloped him. Large rock formations with flowing waterfalls and freshwater ponds underneath them provided the sustenance needed to keep this valley full of vibrant life. And there were stars. Big stars, little stars, stars as far as the eye could see. Lucis had never seen stars mingling with clouds before; it was if the sky danced in perfect harmony for his amusement. A joyous sight to behold.

 "This is absolutely breathtaking. I wish all my brothers could see this."

"Lucis, do you know what this place is and how I came to acquire it?"

 "No, I don't know my lord, but if you would just take a moment and look...."

"Aah, aah, aah...It is rude to enter another person's home and not allow them to speak first. I know you have more manners than that!"

 "Yes, Michael, please tell me more"

"This was the birthplace of man. Can you believe it?" All this beauty and serenity gave to them in their infancy. No strings or conditions. There is so much beauty in the place it almost brings a tear to my eye every morning--I bet you didn't know that, did you?"

 "No, sir, a being of your might reduced to tears is hard to fathom."

"Now you are just humoring me by telling me what I want to hear. There is no need for brown-nosing. I know I can be difficult to work for, even rash and tempered at times, but being here, in this place, makes me whole again."

 "Sometimes, I think, what if man would have never disobeyed GOD? Could both man and angels have coexisted? We are not THAT much different from mankind; sure, we are larger and possess abilities that men do not, but what else really separates us?"

"Well, that's an easy one, Michael, Sin... Sin is what separates us from man. That is why the humans were cast out of paradise."

"Excellent, Lucis, Sin, of course, but original sin did not occur until after Eve was deceived and ate from this tree I now prune. However, have you ever thought why GOD did it? Why tempt such fragile beings in the first place? Did GOD give the race of man free will, knowing that they would use that will to defy him, or to take it a step further since GOD knows all, did he know that Adam and Eve would eat the forbidden fruit, allowing him to cast them out of paradise to toil and suffer for a living."

"No, I do not ponder on such things. Armin told us that to question GOD is dangerous and punishable by death."

"Psst... Armin, such a boy scout. He was definitely the right angel to lead you. He never questions anything even when his own..."

Michael paused

"Never mind. Your accusations are misplaced young warrior, I do not question GOD. I applaud him for what he did. Answer me this, Lucis, how do you know you love the Everlasting?"

"Another easy one, by eradicating evil and protecting the good by the powers he gave me."

"EXACTLY! You know because you would sacrifice your life for him, and if humans are who GOD favors the most, would he not expect the same? The Divine One wants to be SHOWN that you love him. Not trough acts per se but through suffering and sacrifice. You see, we are not so different from man after all. The thing that separates man from us is free will—the freedom to defy GOD. We angels do not have this power.

" When Lucifer came close to harnessing it, he was cast out and thrown into the pit of fire for all eternity. I believe the ability of choice is more powerful than all the powers of the twelve combined."

"I have heard the stories, the battle between you and Lucifer is legendary,"

 "Yes, legendary, but I bet you did not know that Morningstar and I were best friends, did you?"

"You? Best friends with that snake? That cannot be true?"

 "Is that so hard to believe, young warrior? Lucifer was not always the beast we fight today. He was a good warrior with an exceptional singing voice. So good, that he was the only Knight ever removed from duty to serve as the leader of GOD's choir. Boy, did we tease him on that day. His new nickname was choir

boy. How he hated being called that. He and I were inseparable for many years until I noticed a change in him."

"What sort of change?"

 "The sort of change that would ultimately destroy him. No matter how hard I tried to reach him, Lucifer always wanted to more. In the end, it was his lust for power that wrought the great divide."

Michael took a long deep breath as he gazed into the sky for solace and serenity.

 "Now, what brings you to my door, Lucis? Surely, you don't want to hear me ramble on about a past long forgotten."

THE ARCHANGEL TURNED TO FACE LUCIS AND FINALLY NOTICED THREE DEAD ALIEN BODIES CUT TO PIECES LYING IN FRONT OF HIM. IN A PANIC, THE ARCHANGEL SWIFTLY OPENED HIS WINGS AND COVERED THE BODIES. WHEN HE OPENED THEM AGAIN, TO LUCIS'S ASTONISHMENT, THE SPECIMENS WERE NO LONGER THERE. The look on Lucis's face gave Michael all the information he needed.

 "So, you were attacked by aliens while on Earth, yes?"

"Yes, Michael, but how is that possible? Armin, always told us that aliens did not exist."

 "Armin, the Wise, should be wise enough to know that he knows nothing. Tell me, Knight, if GOD can make angels, planets, trees, the ocean, grass, the desert, men, animals, the stars, the sun, and the heavens, surely he can make what we call aliens, yes."

"Well, yes, but."

 "But what? Now, you are beginning to question your Creator."

Lucis quickly closed his mouth and hung his head in shame.

Michael lovingly went to one knee and, with his finger, raised his head so that they could be eye to eye.

 "There is no need for shame, mighty Lucis. We angels are not perfect. The reason you failed against Legion was not that you lacked faith, it was because you lacked humility. To admit that you are flawed brings you more power than you realize. Stop trying to be Lucis, Knight of the Trinity, Master of Light, and just be Lucis. In this, you will be able to harness your true power, with no limitations."

"But Legion warned me..."

 "You would take the word of that despicable demon over me, the Archangel and commander of the armies of heaven! Trust me, Lucis. Trust and believe, and you will be free to unleash your power at will."

"I will trust you, Archangel. Forgive me for my despair,"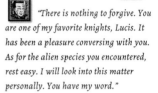

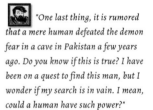 "There is nothing to forgive. You are one of my favorite knights, Lucis. It has been a pleasure conversing with you. As for the alien species you encountered, rest easy. I will look into this matter personally. You have my word."

"Now, if there is nothing else, I have my garden to attend to."

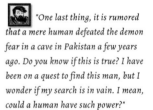 "One last thing, it is rumored that a mere human defeated the demon fear in a cave in Pakistan a few years ago. Do you know if this is true? I have been on a quest to find this man, but I wonder if my search is in vain. I mean, could a human have such power?"

Michael looked at him and smiled, "Continue your search for the truth and remember one thing--all things are possible."

9 | Transgressions of the Favored

"Gunns must die—and he will die at my hands"- Lucis

Tears of anguish, children screaming, and women wailing filled the night air as Lucis entered the city. An all too familiar sound amongst the residents of a border town. The few good people that could not afford to move to greener pastures were subject to all sorts of deviant acts of malevolence from the criminals who now occupied it; that was until the Border Laws were passed by President Rothchild.

Now, no one was safe; criminals, deviate, or otherwise. Local law enforcement cared not for the criminals, outcasts, or 'border-jumping' refugees. Their only job was to clear out dwellings and residents to make room for what the national newspaper proclaimed, "The greatest marvel in border security the world has ever seen."

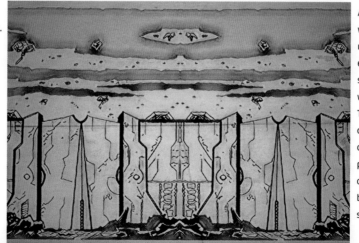

As Lucis gazed upon the wall, he was astonished that for once, the hype was more than just propaganda. The wall stood at least 30 to 40 feet from his estimation and was made of solid steel tinted to a dark green hue. The exterior appeared to be impenetrable with no access stairs or entryways, except for large access elevators that were only opened via eye scan.

At the top of the wall, massive watchtowers with rapid-fire machine guns were constructed, each with border patrolmen strapped with semi-automatic weapons. And the drones... There were military-grade drones everywhere hovering, circling, and monitoring their programmed routes, each covering a defined radius on both sides of the massive structure.

Lucis thought about flying up to inspect one of them, but he did not want to get shot for his trouble.

This is a distraction, he said to himself. *I must stay focused on my mission; I must find Forge and save his soul before it is too late.*

Refocused, Lucis took the appearance of a border patrol lackey and strolled by the dwellings and businesses near the wall. He did not need to wait very long before his search bore fruit.

 *"Bring them out, D-Money. They have had long enough to collect their possessions."*

At long last, the man who stood before him was the very man Lucis had been searching for. The red complexion, long black hair, broad nose, and red bandana was a dead giveaway. Lucis was beside himself; *What should he do? What should he say?* He chose wisdom over emotion and decided he would continue to conceal his true intentions. After all, he needed to see what type of man Forge had become after all these years of searching.

A dark bronze figure cloaked in all black armor came into view, shoving a man twice his size out of what looked to be a small, poorly built residential dwelling. The man did not come willingly, but the pistol D-Money kept beside him kept him in-line, or at least for the smallest of moments.

In an instant, fists flew and teeth as well. The large man pressed his considerable size advantage against the unsuspecting D-Money, and before he knew what had happened to him, his attacker was on top of him, striking him with blow after blow.

To Lucis's surprise, Forge did not make a move towards the man, nor lift a finger to help his colleague. He just stood there with his arms folded like the whole ordeal was boring him.

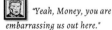 *"Calm down over there, or I will twist this little bitch's neck until I hear a pop,"* a deep voice said as he came near the fray. The man coming near them was a beast of a man, way more massive and muscular than the one getting the upper hand on D-Money. He stood close to 7 feet tall, dressed in what looked like cybernetic gear more than military armor, dragging a little girl no more than 7 or 8, by the top of her head; knees bloody in her attempt to resist.

The man rolled off D-Money, quickly and fell to his knees in compliance. Finally, Forge decided to intervene.

 *"That is enough! Money quit messing around and put the cuffs on this big motherfucker so we can move on to the next house. I don't have all night to watch you get your ass kicked"*

The remark brought a chuckle to the one holding the girl hostage. He decided to chime in.

 *"Yeah, Money, you are embarrassing us out here."*

"Shut the fuck-up, Terminator. He snuck me. I would kick his ass in a straight-up fight,"

blood continued to flow down his mouth and chin. He did not seem to notice.

"Sure, Sure, double-o-seven. I guess you couldn't spy your way out of a good ass-whuppin, huh" Terminator jested.

Forge could not hold his stern face any longer as he laughed out loud to that barb,

"Alright, Alright...how many times have I told you to stop getting wasted before a raid Money? You aren't worth shit to me drunk. Maybe next time you will listen. Now, let's deal with this one and move on. We got ten more houses to evacuate tonight."

Forge's face quickly turned from glee to stone as he looked at the man on his knees sobbing.

"So, what is it going to be, tough guy? Your home or your daughter's life?"

The man pleaded for mercy *"I don't know who you are, but I do know that you are just following orders. Spare my daughter and me, and my home, and I promise I will leave on my own accord. I have a job, a good-paying job if you can just give me thirty more days...."*

"Let me stop you there, big fella. You don't have thirty more days. The cut-off date to move was 2-weeks ago...and about that job of yours, my crew and I have a job as well, and you are making things very, very difficult. Now, I ask again...your home or your daughter's life?"

Lucis was shocked by what he was witnessing. Is this the same man they called 'Demon-Slayer?'

The same man who sacrificed all in the name of what was righteous and holy? He continued to watch intently; in no way was he going to interfere.

The man's head dropped as he squeaked out the words *"My daughter's life. You can take the house, but please spare my daughter."*

Forge placed his hands gently on the top of the man's head and whispered,

"Good decision, let the girl go, T, and for God's sake show a little compassion, you big ape."

Terminator nodded in compliance and bandaged the girl's knees with his first-aid kit before he let her go. All she gave him was a cold sneer in return. Terminator returned the favor with a smirk of his own.

The girl rushed over to hug her father but was stopped abruptly by D-Money, still oozing blood from his mouth and nose.

"Take her to the holding cells. Your father will join you soon, I promise."

Lucis let out a sigh of relief. At last, he had seen a glimpse of the man he thought he would find--one with compassion and mercy. Surely, he could convince him to give up this thug for-hire work and join Lucis in his quest to defeat the Sons of Legion.

"Now, as for you, just sign this form, giving us the rights to your quaint little abode here, and all is well."

As he handed the form over, a sudden gush of spit and blood splashed resting on Forge's face.

"*I hope you are cursed for this, you monster!*" the desperate man exalted loudly as if anyone that mattered could hear him.

Forge's looked at the man with an absolute fire and rage that would make even the most hardened man blink as he put his 9-millimeter Glock to the crown of his head.

 "*Monster? Monster, you say?*"

He scratched his chest, blood dripping from what seemed to be an old wound.

"*No, my friend. I have SEEN real monsters. I have faced real darkness, heart beating out of your chest with death all around you. The stench of piss and shit as men empty themselves in their final moments. I have experienced real terror. Terror, a simple man like you, could never fathom--and what do I get for it in return? You spitting in my face.*"

A SHOT RANG OUT, BLOWING BRAIN MATTER AND BITS OF SKULL OUT THE BACK OF THE MAN'S HEAD AS HE CRUMPLED TO THE GROUND IN A HEAP.

LUCIS HAD JUST SEEN A SMALL GLIMPSE INTO THE FUTURE, HE COULD NOT LET THIS HAPPEN.

IF FORGE GOES TOO FAR... LUCIS THOUGHT.

HE MUST STOP THIS FROM HAPPENING AND STOP IT NOW.

Lucis quickly removed his hand and took a few significant steps back to avoid suspicion. As far as Forge knew, he was just some fat patrolman who was too cowardly to interfere. He made sure to keep it that way. At that moment, Forge realized that his gun was

Lucis moved quickly into action and rested his hand on Forge's shoulder.

 "*I have experienced real terror, terror a simple man like you.... like you...*" Forge shook his head vigorously like he was trying desperately to wake from a dream.

 "*Wait, what was I saying?*"

pointed at the sobbing man's temple.

He came to his senses and holstered the weapon immediately.

"I made your little girl a promise, and I intend to keep it." He grabbed the keys from his belt and released the man from his bondage.

 "You are free to go, but never come back, or I will finish what I started"

The man nodded quickly in compliance. As he turned to walk away, Forge gave him a pause.

 "One last thing," A right-hand haymaker landed squarely on the jaw of the massive man unsuspectedly, knocking him out cold.

To add insult to injury, Forge spat on him as he walked over his unconscious body, put a pen in his hand, and marked an 'X' for his signature.

 "Now you may go," he said with an evil look of satisfaction in his eye.

Lucis shook his head and let out a small chuckle. *Well, it was better than killing the man,* he thought to himself. And besides, his mission is saving Forge, not everyone in this God-forsaken town.

 "You there. Hey, You" Lucis realized Forge was talking to him.

"Uhh, yes. Yes, sir."

 "Pay attention! Take this man over to the holding cells and burn the house while the crew and I take care of the other homes in this area."

"Yes, sir. Absolutely sir, but by whose order should I do this?"

 "By my orders, Patrolman."

"I understand that, sir, but if I may..."

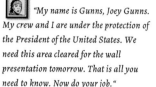 *"My name is Gunns, Joey Gunns. My crew and I are under the protection of the President of the United States. We need this area cleared for the wall presentation tomorrow. That is all you need to know. Now do your job."*

Lucis did as he was told, but not before he blessed the man before putting him in the holding cell. A small act of mercy can go a long way toward his salvation, he thought to himself. As much as Lucis loved humans, he could never determine their final destination. That right resided with GOD and GOD alone. He felt saying a special prayer at least would not hurt his chances--and besides, he had reason to rejoice. Tonight, had been a good night. He now knew where the so-called 'Gunns' was going to be tomorrow. After all his time searching, Lucis could finally devise a plan to get Forge alone with him to ask him the questions that burned in his mind. Lucis was restless but decided patience and rest was the most logical next step. Forge was busy doing the devil's business tonight, he was not in the right mindset for such things. He cloaked himself with invisibility and perched on one of the watch guard towers on top of the wall, choosing to ignore the chaos below of homes burning and women screaming throughout the night.

Stirring and ruckus shouts woke Lucis from his slumber. It takes a lot to wake an angel from a good night's rest. Angels typically sleep for days, when they sleep at all. Lucis was anxious, hoping he did not miss the event altogether due to his prolonged slumber. The sea of people he saw as he looked below gave him comfort that the spectacle was just getting started.

The rumbles and shouts from the crowd could have registered on the Richter scale, as the President's armored limousine pulled up close to the podium. This was not the first time Lucis had seen J.R. Rothchild, in-fact he was at his presidential coronation disguised as a waiter.

He went to all presidential inauguration or dictator ceremonies for that matter. He thought a blessing or two for each leader wouldn't hurt. Whether they accepted into their spirit or not was another matter. Lucis thought of President Rothchild as lukewarm in that department. People that are neither hot nor cold are easily corrupted, he thought to himself. He found that most men of high power suffered from this affliction.

Lucis was rewarded for his patience. Forge himself opened the door for the President and his entourage. *Under the protection of the President indeed,* he thought to himself as he smiled inwardly. From the looks of it, Forge or 'Gunns' had babysitting duty tonight as he hovered close to the Presidents' small boy and wife. From the expression on Forge's face, he did not seem very enthusiastic about it.

The Seventh Spark – Knights of the Trinity

The crowd's persistent roars came to an abrupt halt as the President raised his hand, silencing the crowd. Love him or hate him, he had the group in the palm of his hands and best of all, he knew it. Lucis listened intently at the President's remarks about making the border safe and protecting the country the angel loved so much. The crowd began to chant 'Four more years' as he continued his oratory, raising their fists to the sky.

He had heard enough. Now was not the time to listen to the emptiness of man's promises, he needed focus on the task at hand, and that was to devise a plan to get Forge by himself and show him a better path, a way out of the darkness and into the light that once embraced him. *Mediation and prayer is the key,* he thought to himself. Lucis went out of space and time in hopes that the Everlasting would direct his path to obtain the meeting with Forge that he seeks. GOD works in mysterious ways...

He awoke to the sound a thud as if something or someone had been slammed to the ground. Something was different about him as well. He realized quickly that he was visible, no longer cloaked in secret, however, he was not in pure form.

This form was familiar, he was the old Chinese bum again who roamed the streets of China all those years ago in disgrace. *Things had really come full circle,* he thought to himself.

No time to reminisce, now was the time to figure out what that noise was and what GOD had set before him. To his surprise, it was no other than the red-faced, bandana-wearing Forge lying on the steel floor before him, blood dripping from a fresh head wound.

Lucis decided to stay in his relaxed position and see how this would play out. After all, Forge could not be more potent than angel...then again.

"What the hell do you think you're doing? How did you get on top of the wall without security clearance?"

Lucis rose, his Asian features creasing in a friendly smile, *"Careful there, my friend. You ran over me and fell. Well, actually, I tripped you."*

Forge did not look very amused as he jumped to his feet quickly and aimed his 9-millimeter Glock at the center of Lucis chest

"Who are you, and how did you get here!"

Lucis stood quietly, the same expression of friendship and compassion on his face. After all, what *COULD* he say? He was an angel sent here to protect the realms of men, and he was looking for a partner? Somehow, Lucis did not figure that would go over very well from the look of Forge's face. In fact, his impulse to pull out a gun so aggressively seemed odd. Something must have happened while I was meditating Lucis thought...something terrible.

His thought was interrupted again by a now-familiar voice,

 "Look, Chinatown. I am looking for someone, and you are in my way."

Lucis noticed that Forge was still shaken up about something, but a least had enough sense to holster his gun—even though he continued to come towards him aggressively. Now was not the time to go quietly in the night and slink away. GOD had provided him with this opportunity, he must make the best of it.

Lucis decided then and there that he would not be denied and blocked Forge's way past him. In fact, the two did a little dance as both tried to gain the advantage on one another. By the look on Forge's face, Lucis' new adversary was not in a dancing mood. The angel in disguise figured he would ease the tension by expressing interest in Forge's current mission. Perhaps, this gesture would break the ice.

 "Looking for someone you say," Lucis said calmly while continuing to block Forge's path,

 "well, I know a lot of people, perhaps, I can help you find him?"

The act of grace and courtesy did nothing to calm or change Forge's mood,

"The only thing you are going to find is the hospital if you don't get out of my way. Move or be moved."

And there it is Lucis thought to himself, man's aggression, the answer to ALL their problems, so predictable. The thought brought a smile to his face, exposing his three front teeth and the significant gaps in-between them--a smile only a mother would love.

Lucis countered Forge's aggression with kindness once again.

 "Well, friend, as much as I would like to move, I can't. You see, I'm on a mission, a quest you might say. And I--"

Lucis was rudely interrupted by another outburst of hostility *"Damn it, that's it, now you'll have to talk to Sheila. She has quite a temper, and you've pissed her off."*

What the heck is a Shelia? Lucis pondered. *This guy is beginning*

to irk me. His salvation is upon him, but he is too much of a fool to see it. Has he not noticed that his threats and gestures aren't working?

The reckless talk continued,

"Move now or lose your life Chinaman. I won't ask again."

Wow, Chinaman. He doesn't even have the courtesy to ask my name... and what is up with the racist remarks? Lucis discerned that Forge was not stable and that extreme measures may have to be taken for him to complete his mission. He would try once more to take the high road and said in a calm, soothing tone.

 "As I said before, my friend, I can't do that just yet, how about we sit for a moment and--"

Lucis heard a loud noise and saw the smoke rising from the barrel of the gun pointed at his heart. He looked down at his reflection in the moonlight. A small hole of light peeked through his shadow.

Did Forge just shoot me? Did he just try to kill me?

The thought made him snicker, exposing his not-so pearly whites to Forge once again. *The fool* he thought, *but I shall amuse him.* Lucis stood there defiantly, refusing to fall to the floor, but choosing not to move as well, the same stupid gap-tooth smile planted firmly on his face.

Lucis was getting tired of this charade, it was time to crank it up a notch. To Forge's shock, Lucis grabbed his arm firmly and said in a more definite tone.

 "Wait a minute, my friend. I told you I couldn't let you leave."

Lucis watched with inner glee, as he saw the blood drain from Forge's face. He was scared now, and Lucis knew it. *Maybe soon he will realize the situation he is in and give in to his fate?* Lucis thought, *This can't be real?*

Unbelievable, Lucis thought to himself. This man fought a demon, and he questions why a man can't die by a simple gun wound. Lucis's irritation with Forge was growing—and fast.

 "I told you, I am on a mission, and my mission involves you,"

He continued, not concerned with the look of horror that was now evident on Forge's face.

 "So, you see---"

More shots, more smoke, more holes visible on Lucis's rouge body--the douli he was wearing was knocked clean off from the bullet lodged in his head. This time, his human disguise was not able to withstand the force of the blast, and Lucis fell to the steel ground below him in a heap. This is humiliating, he thought to himself. I have been robbed, stabbed, beaten, and even shot before in my human disguise but not to this extreme.

If I didn't NEED this guy, I would surely make an example out of him.

Lucis's compassion was wearing thin, but then in another outburst of anger, the final straw was broken.

"See you in hell, my friend"

See you in hell? Lucis thought, enraged. *See you in hell!* At that moment, Lucis had concluded that the man that was once a mighty warrior for GOD had died; only this angry, confused, bully named Gunns remained.

Forge must be resurrected, he thought to himself, but first, I must teach this Gunns's character what it means to take on a righteous warrior of the Everlasting.

He quickly rose to his feet, gun wounds prevalent—one in his head, and three in his chest. Lucis was done with the kind buffoon routine, time to take a more direct approach.

"Now that was uncalled for, my friend. You owe me a new body. I really liked this one."

Lucis could now smell the fear. A smell he knew well from anyone who dared face him. He also got an unpleasant whiff of piss and shit expelling from Gunns' body as he stood there, trembling in shock. Lucis continued.

 "I can see you are scared, my friend."

"YOU WILL DIE, CHINAMAN"

In another desperate attempt, Gunns plunged a knife deep into Lucis's now ruined human body. Lucis was ready this time. He grabbed Gunns' hands firmly and held them up so could take an in-depth look into his eyes, which now burned bright with a glowing white light. There was no

turning back now, Lucis would show his true self to Gunns in a way no man has ever seen before. If this man was truly blessed by GOD, he would survive the ordeal. Survive or not, Lucis was beyond reason, beyond mercy. He would kill the man before him and, in his place, would raise a new man; with divine purpose. It was that or Gunns would die in the attempt. Either way, Lucis cared not.

GUNNS MUST DIE, AND HE WILL DIE AT MY HAND.

Lucis gave a sly smile as he put his plan in action.

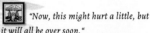 *"My name, friend, is Lucis."*

The transformation was now at hand. Lucis' human confines burst into flame and revealed the warrior angel within in all its glory and splendor.

LUCIS NOW DAWNED A FIERY GOLD AND CRIMSON HALO OF FLAMES OVER HIS HEAD. HIS BODY STRETCHED TO EIGHT-FEET TALL, AND HIS FRAME WAS ADORNED WITH PLATINUM BATTLE ARMOR THAT WOULD RIVAL THE GREEK GODS. HE RELEASED GUNNS FROM HIS GRASP TO UNVEIL HIS HOLY WEAPON. A TWO-HANDED BROADSWORD WITH A JEWEL-ENCRUSTED HANDLE OF DIAMONDS, SAPPHIRES, AND OTHER PRECIOUS RUBIES. HE OUTSTRETCHED HIS MASSIVE WINGS AND LET OUT A BURST OF LIGHT TO SHOW HIS PURE MAGNIFICENCE. A SIGHT THAT MADE GUNNS' KNEES BUCKLE AS HE

TREMBLED IN AWE. TO LUCIS'S SURPRISE, GUNNS DID NOT KNEEL, NOR BEG FOR HIS PITIFUL EXISTENCE. HE JUST STOOD THEIR SCARED, TREMBLING, BUT NOT RELENTING. LUCIS KNEW NOW THAT THIS WAS THE HUMAN THAT DEFEATED LEGION'S SON FEAR. A WARRIOR SPIRIT NEVER DIES, LUCIS THOUGHT TO HIMSELF. PERHAPS THERE IS HOPE FOR HIM AFTER ALL. NOW WAS THE TIME TO FIND OUT.

Lucis's voice boomed in his ascended form.

 "Now, this might hurt a little, but it will all be over soon."

LUCIS'S HOLY FIGURE DEMATERIALIZED INTO WHITE SMOKE. GUNNS BREATHED DEEP AS THE SPIRITUAL ESSENCE OF THE WARRIOR ANGEL SEEPED INTO EVERY ORPHEUS OF HIS BODY. GUNNS SHOOK UNCONTROLLABLY, THEN COLLAPSED IN A HEAP ON THE COLD STEEL FLOOR.

10 The Angel and the Lion

"I've felt this presence before, a son of Legion is here" - Lucis

That's better. What an angry guy.

Inside Forges' unconscious mind, Lucis entered his eternal soul, seeking what could be salvaged. The atmosphere was cold, damp, and smelled of rot. Every footstep crunched and crackled, as though he trod upon shells crushed beneath the soles of his armored boots. Lucis squatted down to investigate:

SINS...

He read, in those bits and pieces, every sinful act Forge had committed in his clandestine activities. Demonic cherubs feasted on the wickedness encased in

Forge's soul with insatiable gluttony. From what he saw, Forge had amassed enough immoral deeds to feed an entire population of demons for a long stint. As the specters gorged themselves on constructs of Forges' misdeeds, they swelled, then belched out a smaller version of themselves—a new generation recycling on the buffet of sin that was Forge's soul. Engrossed in their vile feast, the apparitions were slow to recognize Lucis's presence. When they did, he felt the force of their perpetual hunger and ravenous greed. He dismissed it. The divine glow of holiness would protect him.

The gloom around him grew thick and pressed against him. Though he remained surrounded by a thin layer of divine illumination, he needed more light to see where this dark path led. With naught but a flicker of will, Lucis strengthened his luminance. The golden glow penetrated the dense, rotten darkness. The demons shrank back, despite their hunger and greed. They were no match for the light of righteousness, and they knew it.

Lucis had ascended, no longer bound by the time constraints of his gift. A feat no other Knight had accomplished, not even Armin. He was anxious to see the prude look on his face when he told him. Those ambitious actions would have to wait. Lucis pressed his mind back to a singular focus,

saving Forge from his sins and eternal fate and redeeming his spirit as the man unknowingly did for him.

He paused to consider what the detritus beneath his feet meant. Squatting down, the angel examined them more carefully a second time.

The horde of minions feasted on the recycled remains of old and new sins. While these demons were formable for weaker souls, Lucis knew it would take more than a few minor soul suckers to expel the light from a man such as this. The further Lucis ventured into the depths of Forge's soul, the more he knew something way more sinister and fouler was at work here.

Lucis had a moment of revelation.

I'VE FELT THIS THING BEFORE, I KNOW ITS PRESENCE...IT IS A SIN, A DEADLY SIN. A SON OF LEGION IS HERE, AND ITS WREAKING HAVOC. I NEED TO DO SOMETHING FAST BEFORE ALL GOODNESS IS EXTINGUISHED FROM THIS POOR SOUL, LUCIS PONDERED.

He pressed on, speculating as to how one particular sin had grown so powerful. Repetition was the most likely, as repetition built a sin's strength, especially when it was rewarded.

The small demons infesting Forge shrank from the angel's brilliance. Those that did not move quickly enough sizzled to harmless ash when touched by the divine light. Anxious to preserve their miserable

existence, they scattered like vermin, leaving him a clear path. He ignored them as he marched onward, for they did not merit his attentiveness. The more he trudged down the construct of Forge's soul, the thicker the putrid miasma grew. Lucis pressed on, his steps becoming heavy as though wading through neck-deep water. The hollow sound of a steady drip added to the effect.

Wearying, Lucis snagged one of the evil cherubim's cowering in a corner.

"You there," he said, trapping the demon within a fence of light. *Tell me where I can find the alpha demon, one of Legion's offspring. You know of whom I speak."*

The small apparition trembled with good reason, but it feared something more than Lucis.

"Who--who is this of which you speak?" it squeaked. *"I know nothing. Even if I did, I could not speak truly..."*

"Answer me!" Lucis snapped, the crack of his deep voice and threatening tone reverberated throughout the hollow soul.

"You do know the penalty of lying to one such as I?"

The spirit attempted to melt into the damp, filth-encrusted wall behind it, but it could not break the angel's gaze and therefore hide in the choking darkness. Only truth would yield freedom.

The spirit pointed toward a small covering and grunted as truth-force itself painfully from its throat,

"There. He is there."

Lucis thanked him and headed in the direction indicated by the evil spirit. He forbore to reward the demon with the edge of his sword, knowing that the poisonous taint of truth would deliver a slow, painful death to it. Perhaps, he thought, the sincerity might infect other demons and make the eventual job of savaging Forges' soul a little easier.

"Wait, God's pet!" the little demon snarled. Lucis paused but did not turn back. The fiend babbled, *"He has been feeding. You are one, and he is many. Powerful. You cannot win. Your light is weak against our darkness. You cannot win. You--"*

"Hold your tongue, foul creature!" Lucis's voice rumbled through the thick, putrid darkness. *"I am of the light. I bring God's justice and swift retribution. A Knight of Trinity assembled by the Archangel himself!"*

THE GROUND SHOOK. DEMONS NEAR AND FAR TREMBLED IN TERROR. ANNOYED BY THE INTERRUPTION, SEARING BEAMS OF WHITE LIGHT SHOT FROM LUCIS'S EYES AND STRUCK THE IMPERTINENT INCUBUS. THE CREATURE SHRIEKED AND THEN EXPLODED IN A FOUL PUFF OF BLACK SMOKE AND GREASY ASH. A SHADOW OF THE IRREGULAR SHAPE OF IT REMAINED BURNED INTO THE WALL BEHIND WHERE IT HAD COWERED.

Lucis trekked on, irritated with himself, and doubting that he had successfully compelled the nasty little spirit into speaking truthfully. *'Little liars, all of them,'* he thought to himself. Treated to the angel's display of power, the lesser demons infesting Forges' soul retreated before him, giving the angel of war plenty of room to find whatever he sought.

Already tired from trudging through this contaminated soul, Lucis knew he would get no help from this sinful lot, and to continue to search aimlessly was a futile effort.

Lucis had a revelation,

"I must call out the darkness and bring it into the light."

Lucis drew his sword. Embossed with golden light that filled the unconscious host's soul in its entirety, scattering the evil vermin who could not hide from its glow. He shouted,

"I am the truth and light. All evil shall tremble before my brilliance"

A flash of light illuminated Forge's soul leaving no crack or crevice unlit. The move proved useful as he heard a sinister voice in the distance

"Pretty, pretty light."

"Very, very bright."

"Pretty, pretty light."

"Must see this sight."

AN OMINOUS FIGURE CAME INTO THE PRESENCE OF LUCIS'S PURE WHITE GLOW.

THE ANGEL'S GAZE FLICKERED WITHOUT EMOTION OVER THE MAGNIFICENT FIGURE OF A BEING WITH A LION'S HEAD. A GOLD CROWN RESTED UPON THE THICK MANE. THE LION'S FACE WAS STRANGELY ELONGATED, ITS SHARP FANGS PROTRUDING OVER THE LOWER LIP. THE BODY RESEMBLED A HUMAN FRAME CARVED FROM STONE, GOLDEN IN COLOR, AND GLEAMING AS THOUGH INFUSED BY THE PRECIOUS METAL. LONG CLAWS PROTRUDED FROM THE CREATURE'S LARGE HANDS AND FEET. A LION'S TAIL SWISHED BEHIND THE NAKED FIGURE, WHICH BORE NO REPRODUCTIVE ORGANS.

Lucis inclined his head in wary greeting, he *HAD SEEN* this demon before. He quickly remembered where.

"Pride, son of Legion, we meet again."

The demon approached, meeting Lucis's intense stare with his own red-eyed glare. More sing-song words uttered in a soft, menacing rasp followed:

"Angel, angel, can't you see?"

"This pitiful, putrid soul belongs to me."

"Go away, go away."

"Your glorious bright light cannot stay."

"Do not speak your nonsense to me, demon. You are boastful, a braggart."

The angel studied the demon's face, perfect, with no marks or scars from battle. The sinister wraith was draped in all sorts of luxurious trappings—a testament to his indulgence in the exquisite things men offered freely in exchange for their souls. Large diamonds tipped each point on his circlet crown that rested on top of his head. Thick rope gold chains hung from his neck and wrists. In fact, his entire body appeared to be fused in solid gold, indeed a magnificent sight of opulence for one to behold.

He has been busy sucking the souls of the rich and famous no doubt, Lucis thought to himself.

He stepped forward, squaring his shoulders and presenting a brave front.

Pride spoke

True, true, all is true."

"You know me, but I don't know you."

"You may not know me, beast, but you know my kind. I am one of the twelve. I am a Knight of the Trinity, Lucis, bringer of Light part of the Everlasting Order ordained by GOD himself," Lucis identified himself.

The lion's proud sneer twisted into a snarl and retorted in iambic pentameter:

"The Order? Here inside such a weak soul?"

"His spirit is failing, his faith too old."

"He cannot be saved."

"Few have tried."

"He is consumed by the lion."

"He is overtaken by pride."

Lucis rebutted against the demon's doggerel and responded in kind

"You dare stand in the way of God's will! There are none who could give you this authority, not even Lucifer himself."

Pride's rasping voice rang with defiance.

"Never would I make that mistake."

"God is not here; he sent you in his place."

"Try if you must and try you will."

"Pride will not fall; the Lightbringer I'll kill."

A lion's mighty roar erupted from the demon's toothy maw and shook the ground upon which they stood. The power of it stunned the angel. He instinctively raised his hands to cover his ears against the cacophony. The roar subsided, and Lucis recovered his sword, disallowing embarrassment from affecting his mission.

The ground rumbled again, as Pride gave a twisted smile but did not speak. Lucis looked behind him and saw ruse for what it really was. The demon's roar called hordes of demon cherubims to him, awaiting his instruction. Lucis realized he had once again underestimated the cunning of darkness, a mistake he thought he could never make again.

WITH A ROAR OF HIS OWN, LUCIS LUNGED TOWARD PRIDE. HIS GREATSWORD FLAMED WITH HOLY FIRE AS HE SLASHED AND SWIPED. THE POWERFUL DEMON COUNTERED WITH GRACEFUL AND DEADLY ACCURATE SWIPES FROM HIS RAZOR-SHARP CLAWS. HIS LARGER FORM AND EXTENDED REACH FORCED LUCIS TO ADVANCE CLOSER TO THE DEMON'S BODY THAN HE WOULD HAVE PREFERRED. PRIDE HOOKED HIS LETHAL CLAWS INTO THE ANGEL'S SIDE, RIPPING THROUGH HIS SILVERY ARMOR AND SPIRIT FLESH. ROARING WITH PAIN AND FURY, LUCIS REDOUBLED HIS EFFORTS, LEAVING BLACK, SMOKING WELTS ON THE DEMON'S NO-LONGER-PERFECT BODY. THE BATTLE RAGED ON, NEITHER QUITE GAINING THE UPPER HAND. WHEN LUCIS PRESSED HIS ADVANTAGE, PRIDE'S MINIONS WOULD CLIMB ON THE ANGELIC WARRIOR AND SLASH AND BITE WITH THEIR SHARP TEETH AND CLAWS. LUCIS WOULD THEN PULSE PURE WHITE, DIVINE LIGHT, WHICH BLASTED THEM AWAY AND BLINDED PRIDE SO HE COULD AGAIN RETURN TO THE FRAY.

THE INJURIES SUSTAINED BY EACH OF THEM TOOK THEIR TOLL. LUCIS'S SPIRIT DIMMED FROM PURE WHITE TO DINGY GRAY WITH THE IMPACT OF EVIL TOUCHING HIS SPIRIT BODY. PRIDE'S GLEAMING GOLD HIDE TURNED DULL, ITS LEFT ARM SPASMED WHERE IT LAY ON THE FLOOR, AND A GREAT GASH SLICE SIZZLED ACROSS ITS CHEST. LUCIS LEVELED THE DRIPPING EDGE OF HIS SWORD ALONG PRIDE'S THICK THROAT AND PRESSED THE BLADE SO THAT IT PARTED THE SKIN. BLOOD WELLED UP AND CHARRED ALONG WITH THE SILVERY METAL. THE DEMON SANK TO ONE KNEE, THE SWORD NEVER WAVERING FROM ITS IMMINENT THREAT TO SLIDE ALL THE WAY THROUGH ITS NECK.

"It's over," Lucis grunted as he gasped for air and tried to hide the weary tremors in his arms and legs.

"You have lost, Pride. Darkness can never defeat the light."

The demon's cuts bled gray ichor; its vigor diminished. The golden crown tilted at a crazy angle, cracked and missing several of its diamonds, which had also faded in brilliance. One eye had swollen shut. It raised its remaining hand, the claws sheared off from an ill-considered tussle against that divine blade. With defeat imminent, Pride could not back down.

It was Pride, and Pride did not admit defeat.

"Oh, great warrior, I must disagree.

Darkness has defeated light before, for all the world to see.

My father Legion beat an ancient angel of old.

He sent the angel in hiding as legend is told.

This is the reason I grew so strong. Feasting on innocents that did not know right from wrong.

All this time gorging on sin, unchecked and unchallenged, where has the Order been? Running and hiding? afraid to fight?"

No more saving souls no more of GOD's light.

A mere human faced terror and chose to be bold. He killed my brother, to protect his, so I took his soul."

The response rocked Lucis to his core. After all this time, it was his fault that Forge had become the horrible human being he is today. *'All because of my cowardice,'* he thought to himself, lowering his mighty great sword. This provided the opportunity Pride needed to escape his grasp.

Prides mighty paw slashed at Legion once again, exposing flesh as most of the metal from his armor has been shredded from the battle. Lucis took a few steps back, wincing in pain. Pride took advantage. *THE DEMON LET OUT ANOTHER THUNDEROUS ROAR THAT REVERBERATED THROUGH FORGE'S SOUL IN A LAST ATTEMPT TO WIN THE DAY. THE REMAINING EVIL SPIRITS RESPONDED, CRAWLING AND SLITHERING UP THE ALPHA DEMON'S BODY LIKE INNUMERABLE SPIDERS AND SERPENTS. THEY POURED DOWN HIS GAPING MOUTH AND SACRIFICED*

THEMSELVES IN UNTHINKING OBEDIENCE. PRIDE SWALLOWED THEM WHOLE, GORGING ON THEIR EVIL, ABSORBING THEIR PUNY STRENGTH INTO HIS OWN, COMPOUNDED COUNTLESS TIMES LIKE SNOWFLAKES PILING INTO A SNOWDRIFT.

Lucis watched in disgust as the demon's belly swelled and wondered whether Pride thought to escape punishment by destroying itself. He watched as the beast grew, first its stomach, then the bloating surged through its chest and limbs. No longer the masculine beauty topped by a lion's head, the ponderous demon rose to its grossly swollen feet and grinned with extreme malevolence.

Lucis continued to watch, continued to hold his sword ready, though his arms and legs burned with exhaustion. Pride opened its mouth again and bellowed, though Lucis did not know whether from pain or frustration or anger. The aberration's body rippled and bulged with gruesome sounds of bone cracking and muscle tearing. The severed arm regenerated. The smoking and charred cuts healed. The claws grew back, as sharp and pointy as ever.

The angel realized what had happened and lunged before the demon's golden color resumed its bright gleam. The weight of his sword dragged at his arm. His injuries left him slow and sluggish.

THE DEMON DODGED, EASILY AVOIDING THE KILLING BLOW AND COUNTERATTACKED. THE DEMON'S FIERCE, SHARP FANGS SANK DEEPLY INTO LUCIS'S NECK.

CORRUPTION SEEPED FROM THE DEMON'S BODY INTO THE ANGEL'S, ALMOST COMPLETELY EXTINGUISHING THE DIVINE GLOW. AS THE BEAST CHEWED, LUCIS STRAINED TO RAISE HIS SWORD, BUT HIS WEAK HANDS DROPPED THE MIGHTY WEAPON. AS HE FADED, HE ATTEMPTED ONE LAST TIME TO AVERT HIS OWN DEATH. Lucis's voice now rasped as he appealed to the demon's vanity, using the name it could not resist.

"Pride, demon, I say your name."

"Are you not boastful? Are you not vain?"

Compelled by the expression of its name, the demon released its hold on Lucis to speak.

"My name, my name. You called my name. I am boastful, I am vain."

"Are you certain? Is that plain?"

Lucis whispered, every word an enormous effort as his dwindling strength faded quickly.

"You are flawed. You are not the same."

"Your claw is missing. How can that be?"

"You are perfect. You are vanity."

AFFRONTED BY THE ANGEL'S MOCKERY, PRIDE TOOK A FEW STEPS BACK AND EXAMINED HIS NEWLY DECLAWED HAND. CONFUSION AND DISBELIEF TWISTED ITS FEATURES AS IT ATTEMPTED TO UNDERSTAND HOW IT HAD LOST ITS PERFECTION. THE INCONGRUITY OF BEING CALLED PERFECT WHILE EVIDENCE OF IMPERFECTION COULD NOT BE DENIED POSED A RIDDLE IT COULD NOT DEFEAT. THE LION TWISTED UPON ITSELF, SEEKING TO RESTORE IS PERFECTION.

RELEASED FROM THE DEMON'S UNHOLY GRIP, LUCIS RAISED HIS SWORD WITH THE LAST DROPS OF HIS STRENGTH AND SWUNG, LETTING THE BLADE'S MASSIVE WEIGHT DO THE WORK FOR HIM.

THE DIVINE SWORD SLICED THROUGH THE DEMON'S NECK WITH A HARSH SIZZLE AND A MEATY THUD. THE DEMON'S HEAD FELL TO THE FLOOR, ITS FACE FROZEN IN A RICTUS OF SURPRISE, RED EYES STILL GLOWING AS IT ROLLED.

Lucis, dizzy from his wounds and fading energy, rose to his feet. He knew what he must do. Perhaps the time of angels protecting man was over, he thought to himself as he prepared himself for the task at hand. After all, a mere mortal had defeated Fear, endured the inner torture of Pride to boot, and survived to the terror of an angel entering his soul. Perhaps... just perhaps, saving *THIS* man was the key to planet Earth's perseverance. A lofty ambition, no doubt, but the only one he could hope for at this point. Lucis had defeated Pride; however, the cost meant his life was forfeit as well. He no longer sparkled with brilliant light, his spirit was dull and grey, forever tainted from the injuries obtained in the conflict for Forge's soul. Restoring this man's morality was the least he could do, one last good deed to add to his legacy—

THE FINAL SACRIFICE OF THE LIGHTBRINGER, THE 21ST WARRIOR ANGEL OF THE EVERLASTING ORDER, KNIGHT OF THE TRINITY, MASTER OF THE BROADSWORD, AND PROTECTOR OF THE HUMAN REALM OF EARTH.

KNEES SHAKING FROM BENEATH HIM AND SPIRIT FADING INTO DARKNESS, LUCIS LET OUT ONE LAST BATTLE CRY AS HIS BODY EXPLODED INTO BRILLIANT GLOWING WHITE LIGHT.

11 | Beginning of the End

"He was the best of us" - Armin

No one knew how to start.

The breeze from paradise was light, but the hearts were heavy. Lucis, bringer of Light, one of the best of them, was dead, killed protecting the realm he loved. Now came time for them to pass final judgment upon one they all respected and admired. Even the always opinionated Absolution was subdued, staying close by Michael's side. The loss was especially brutal to him as Lucis was the only one in the Order to treat him as an equal and not an outcast as the others did.

Armin cleared his throat, the silence broken, he continued

"Surely, no one here can deny Lucis's greatness, he was the best of us. A gifted warrior, compassionate leader, and counselor to each and every one of us" "But I cannot give him my vote for ascension."

Sounds of contentment began to surface from the statement.

Armin pushed on quickly to quell the uprising.

"Hear me, brothers. The future holds infinite possibilities. Can we be certain there is no one greater to claim the title of the Ascended One? My spirit tells me that there is someone greater still, and I am bound by honor to obey my own heart in this matter. We all remember Ophilius the Great. His name is still legend amongst these halls. However, patience and wisdom prevailed, and the final vote was not cast."

"It was only later that a mere scout, Absolution, was able to break his demon count. Imagine how foolish we would have been if we did not have the gift of time on our side? I say we once again, we make the hard choice and deny passage to brother Lucis for the sake of more celebrated Knights to come. Brothers, I ask you, who is with me?"

Armin paused to assess the mood. He was dismayed by the looks of contentment in most of his guild. Stevyn, Lucis' best companion, was inconsolable, repeatedly leaving his brethren for moments of solitude and reflection for the one he loved dearly. Even Rupin, ever by his side, could not provide much comfort.

"Brothers, I know emotions are high, but remember, I am the wisest of you all. Trust that I know best."

The grumbles from indecision festered and boiled over. The debate for the Lucis, the Lightbringer, had begun.

Raj, the Ancient spoke first,

"No one can deny Lucis's bravery and position on this council, but he died saving one man, not the planet he swore to protect. I am with Armin. I say there a is a mightier warrior to come."

Roars of approval of Raj's words filled the air.

Jewel rolled her eyes. No one, not even the mysterious Raj was going to tell her how to think

"WHO HERE COULD MATCH THE FURY OF LUCIS' BROADSWORD? I TRIED SEVERAL TIMES AND FAILED IN EACH ATTEMPT."

"WHO HERE GAVE BETTER ADVICE THAN LUCIS? HE SAVED MY BUTT COUNTLESS TIMES ON PLANET NOVA BY HELPING ME MAKE THE RIGHT DECISIONS".

HAZAH!

HAZAH!

"I RESPECT ARMIN, BUT MY SACRIFICE AS A WARRIOR KNIGHT GIVES ME THE RIGHT TO CHOOSE. WHY MUST WE ALWAYS FOLLOW HIS INSTRUCTION LIKE A WHIPPED DOG? STAND-UP FOR ONCE AND LET YOUR TRUE VOICE HEARD."

The Legendary Warrior, Lucis the Lightbringer, The Brilliant Glow of the Everlasting

Years of Service : 1,678 years

# of Demons Slain : 28,356

Battles of Note:
- Defeated OZ the Defiler in single combat (battle lasted two-man years)
- Slayed Valefor the Cruel & Abyss at the same time
- Killed the Pride Lion a child of Demon Lord Legion
- Respected Choir Leader

Weapon of Choice : Two-handed Broadsword (which he carried in one hand)

Favorite Move: Holy Light

Favorite Food : Noodles

Favorite Phrase: Perhaps

The council was in full throat now with cheers from the rousing speech. No one could deny the truth in Jewel's words. More began to make their case.

Stevyn chimed in.

 *"Leader, Warrior, Counselor, Friend. All these things describe my cohort Lucis. His battle with the demon knight OZ the Defiler was one of legend."* Stevyn cleared his throat and breathed deep. He knew his next statement would not be well received,

"However, I have also seen fear overtake him. The same fear that has overtaken me at times. I wonder if the chosen one, anointed among us all, will fear anything. Therefore, I cannot cast my vote for him, nor myself for that matter. As much as it breaks my heart, Lucis is not the chosen one." Stevyn quickly excused himself, tears flowing from his cheeks. He was not interested in hearing the opinions of his guild; he said his peace, now all that was left was to mourn his brother-in-arms. Zane, the Vigilant, took exception to Stevyn's remarks,

"Preposterous! Are we to believe that there is some angel yet to come who does not know fear? To not know fear, is to not know caution or restraint. Do we really want that sort of brute as the example of what a true warrior is? I cast my vote for Lucis. The best of us all. Who is with me?"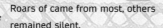

Roars of came from most, others remained silent.

Clandor, the newest of the Order, could no longer hold his tongue.

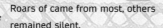 *"Brothers, I know that I have only been a knight for less than a decade, but I must say that Lucis was the one knight I admired when I was just a scout under Stevyn's training. The stories my master told me of Lucis's bravery and courage stays with me and encourages me to be the best Knight I can be. For that, I am eternally grateful. However, I cannot cast my vote for him. The reason is simple. My youth affords me to see things from a different perspective—all scouts dream of becoming the legendary knight, the one who will live forever. If we vote for Lucis, it may be just. Still, it will also take away MY right to earn this honor, as well as all other Knights behind me. I don't know if I would be the warrior I am today without that motivation. Therefore, I must vote nay."*

"Sit down, rookie!" shouted Gaudfridus, *"Grown folks are talking."*

Clandor quickly took his seat, beet red from embarrassment. The rousing debate went on for weeks, much longer than the last gathering for the fallen knight Artemus. Armin did his best to keep things civil, getting assistance occasionally from Michael when tensions started to boil over. Getting a unanimous vote on either side proved to be quite the ordeal. Three months passed in human days, and the campaign against Lucis was getting quite the push from Armin, Raj, Stevyn, and Anisau. . After several raucous debates, three fights, and two all-out brawls, Lucis had two votes for and ten against. Zane was steadfast in his decision, and Jewel's contrary nature was always contentious.

Raj spoke up again in another attempt to sway his brethren.

"*Brothers, I say again, for as long as I have known Armin, he has never led us astray. We must trust his judgment without question.*"

Jewel rolled her eyes so hard they might have left her sockets. "*Fine. I am ready to get this over with. I cast my vote against Lucis for inclusion into the First Realm of Heaven. May he and GOD forgive me.*"

Absolution, devastated by the loss of his only friend, looked deep into the eyes of Zane. It was the look of despair. He could see that the one they call the Vigilant had given up hope and would soon cave to the others. *I cannot let this happen*, Absolution thought to himself. If he did not stand for his friend now, how could he ever live with himself? Absolution was an outsider. Only a knight could cast a vote for Ascension for another knight. It was not his place to intervene in matters of the Order. Yet he felt compelled to support the only knight who treated him as an equal. He could no longer hold his tongue, despite the code.

"*Anointed Knights, the Everlasting's chosen, should you obey just because the great Armin says so? Is HE your GOD now? Forgive me if I do not genuflect.*"

The warriors stared at him, Gaudfridus choking on his ale as silence swept the room.

Armin was furious.

"*Absolution! I will not tolerate blasphemous comments. I was ordained to lead. I did not choose this station, nor did I want it. I am sure Michael has told you the story of the last angel who proclaimed to his creator's equal. His fate and the fate of his followers were sealed forever in eternal fire. How dare you accuse me of the same?*"

Absolution, overcome by emotion, interrupted abruptly.

"*You want the glory for yourself! Admit it! Admit it now and give up this farce of a debate. Lucis was to only in the Order who didn't care about all your needless rules and procedures; he cared about something greater! Now, you want to take away his right to everlasting life for your own glory and self-preservation.*"

Armin stood up and approached Absolution.

"*To insinuate that I would break an oath that I made to the ALMIGHTY for my own personal gain is an insult. An insult to me and an insult to the Order. An insult, worthy of death.*"

"*Go for it! I almost beat you as a teenager, I would surely destroy you now.*"

Armin smirked,

"*You may be a fool, but I am not. You are under Michael's charge, his personal ward. I would not dare to insult the Archangel over something so petty. Besides, scouts are not worth my time.*"

"*Another word from your shrill, nasal voice, and I will remove your head from your shoulders!*"

"*You want my head, come and take it. Let's finish what you started centuries ago. The others may fear you, but I do not.*"

The two warriors rushed at each other in a fevered pace—Armin with his two master swords and Absolution with his Warhammer.

"ENOUGH!"

Michael appeared between the two of them. Armin and Absolution quickly lowered their weapons in obedience.

> "IS THIS WHAT LUCIS WOULD HAVE WANTED? HE WAS VERY FOND OF BOTH OF YOU, AS I RECALL. STOP THIS MADNESS, AND LET'S HONOR LUCIS WITH AN OFFERING OF LOVE AND RESPECT FOR ONE ANOTHER."

Armin and Absolution dropped their weapons and hung their heads, both ashamed at the spectacle they caused. This was a time of reflection and celebration of the life of a great warrior. Lucis would chastise them both for acting like squabbling children.

Armin spoke first to ease the tension.

"Out of respect for Lucis, I can let this insult go if you can relinquish your harsh feelings toward me. Come join us for what is sure to be our greatest memorial service and tournament of heroes ever. I will even give you the honor of sitting with us in the Oracle, with Michael's blessing, of course."

Michael gave a slight nod in agreeance.

Absolution's harsh grimace transformed into a smile as he would finally be included as one of the Order for the proceedings. His one wish had come true, he would be one of them, who cared if it was only for a fortnight.

12 Percival's Sacrifice

"If GOD doesn't kill you for your blasphemy, I will"- Armin

Have a beer will ya. It's quite tasty" Gaudfridus told Clandor.

"As much as I would like to, I'd rather not drink today, have a job to do, you know," Clandor responded.

"No worries, boy, a few rounds of this stuff won't harm you. I think the humans drink this elixir to help them focus--or at least that is what Lucis told me,"

Gaudfridus said, secretly snickering to himself. He meant to get the new guy drunk tonight...I mean, how else could you genuinely get to know someone until they have told a few drunken stories. Artemus was Gaudfridus's best friend, so he figured Clandor would be a suitable replacement. Clandor naivety and desire to be liked soon succumbed to Gaudfridus' influence, and the two were drunk in no time, singing,

and telling stories with raucous laughter. Armin kept his word. This was the largest and best feast to date. All types of roasted meats, vegetables, and desserts were served up and quickly disposed of. The music played for hours. Everyone got a kick out of Berlot and Anisau trying his best to do what the humans on Earth realm called 'break dancing', while Raj and Jewel tried to 'boot scoot boogie'. Michael roared with laughter, so amused that snot bubbles shot out of his nose. Even Armin and Absolution were getting along; the ample amount of what Earth called 'spirits' being served helped. At feasts end, bitter rivals at the start of the day were now standing arm and arm chanting warrior songs they learned as kids.

The two were passed out in the corner together when the one-week festival for the Lucis, the Lightbringer concluded.

The angels awoke the next day to headaches from too much ale and excitement about the events to come. The 277th Tournament of Heroes was about to commence. Everyone presented their challengers. It was tradition that each scout donned their full armor for their introduction to the Order. There are a lot of side wagers made on these fights, and it was bad form for any knight to see any weakness in a contestant before the tournament started. This was tradition, and tradition was everything.

 "Gaudfridus, you look lovely today," Raj spoke in sarcasm as he saw the drunken warrior barely make it to his seat.

"Aww, shut your beak, Raj."

Reimund and Berlot also sat in their seats, woozy from a night of revelry.

 "Too much to drink, brother?"

"Not enough."

Jewel and Stevyn then made their way to their seats and started small talk.

 "Couldn't sleep yesterday, the memory of Lucis's passing still crowds my thoughts."

"Ahh, girl, it'll pass, especially with these delightful spirit drinks from Earth realm. I can't remember a thing last night."

'Or any other night, drunken fool' Jewel thought to herself as she just nodded her head in response

Absolution was the first one to his seat, abuzz with excitement. He would not pass up the chance to see a Tournament up close.

To his surprise, not only did Armin keep his word, he took a seat right beside him as the tournament began.

Unlike the previous tournament, this one was a short affair. Three days, in fact. The shortest competition in remembrance or at least since official records of the event were recorded by Armin. Gaudfridus scout, Ox, won by a landslide, easily defeating his opponents with his mighty battle-axe. The spectacle made Gaudfridus as proud as a peacock, his chest protruding out of his golden armor as he did a little dance in front of his seat. The final match was done. Ox

would be crowned a Knight of the Trinity, the new bringer of light. Out of all of GOD's many gifts, this one was coveted and respected by all his brethren.

"I told you my boy would win. He is the best with a battle-axe since...since, well me, I guess. Steven, Jewel, and Raj, you owe me 75 demons. Pay up now, don't dottle--and I want premium quality, no weaklings."

You could see the disgust on their faces as all three paid in full. Gaudfridus did another little dance while the transactions were being made, that made them all smile. After all, a bet is a bet, and no one dared to break the rules of the tournament for the penalty for such action was certain death.

After the ceremony of remembrance for the fallen scouts, it was time to crown the champion. Armin, overcome with respect for the victor, allowed Gaudfridus to do the honors as he watched beside Absolution and Michael.

"Truly, the Everlasting has blessed your ax this day. Take off your helm and let us welcome you properly as our new brother in arms."

The scout unburdened himself of his helmet to reveal his face.

Silence and confusion gripped the Order. Whispering and murmuring could faintly be heard as the group huddled together. Finally, Gaudfridus spoke to break the silence

"What kind of a joke is this? Where is Ox, the Mighty? This is NOT the scout that is pledged to my service. Who is this IMPOSTER, and how did he get my scouts greaves and armor?"

The murmuring and whispers continued. No one could answer the riddle put before them. Gaudfridus continued his inquiry,

"I ask again, who are you, son? Who are you pledged to? Where is Ox? Did you kill him and take his armor so you could be in the tournament? Answer me, boy, or I will surely have your head!"

Absolution was the first to speak up.

"Stand down, Gaudfridus. There is no need to threaten the boy. He is innocent in this. I am the one who put him up to it."

 *"What! Why? Why would you betray ME, Bane! We are comrades I have always spoken highly of you to the Order. You know this."*

"I assure you that you were not betrayed, Gaudfridus. Ox is safe and asleep in his bed; I saw to that personally. If anything, I tried to save you the embarrassment when I found him in a drunken stupor laying in his own piss. Some angels just can't hold their liquor."

A few knights chuckled at Absolution's remarks. Gaudfridus grey complexion turned beet red from the embarrassment; he quickly took his seat and made no further objection.

Absolution continued,

"As for the man before you, his name is Percival. I have been training him ever since he had the strength to hold a shield. He has been a pet project of mine if you will. To see if my ward could compete with scouts trained by the legendary knights of the Order. And since I know you stiffs would NEVER allow Percival to enter the tournament officially, I took advantage of the situation and disguised him as Gaudfridus's entry. My ward wiped the floor with your so-called chosen ones, so once again, I have proven that your silly rules are obsolete and pointless. Apologies for the deception, but I think the results speak for themselves"

The knights were speechless... there was an uncomfortable silence; the kind of silence that generally meant terrible consequences were forthcoming. The Order locked hands in defiance and began chanting in a dialect unknown to man or any other being for that matter. The chant got louder and louder until it was deafening.

Armin raised his hand sharply, and the chanting stopped. He looked over to Absolution. It was a look of pity and guilt. As much as he did not like Bane, he did not want to see him hurt. Duty and honor-bound Armin; he was the leader, and he had to obey the law. Out of the many times he did not want to lead, this was by far the worst. Only Armin knew that Absolution had made a grave error in judgment by entering this boy into the tournament....and this mistake

would cost the young ward his life.

Armin took a deep breath and raised one of his master's swords to the sky.

 "By the light of the Order and the Code of the Trinity, I deem the 277th tournament of champions forfeit. The rules of engagement have been broken."

"WHAT? My scout won fair and square. Besides, what will happen to Lucis's seat?"

Armin continued, acting as he did not hear Absolution's plea.

"The rules state that Lucis's seat will remain open for a period of one thousand years. This will allow the Order to time to train new scouts and prepare for a new tournament. Until that time, no new Knights can be initiated into twelve. For the first time since our inception, we will have no twelfth knight. These are rules of the Order according to Article 1257 Section 2."

Armin stared down Absolution,

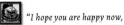 *"I hope you are happy now, Bane! Your insolence has finally broken our way of life, just like I KNEW you would"*

Absolution ignored the slight and continued to plead his case *"Percival worked hard for this; this is madness. Can't he just take Lucis's place until a new tournament can be held? What is the harm? He is a more than capable fighter. You all witnessed his strength. The boy detests evil just as much as I do! LISTEN TO REASON AND DAMN THE ARTICLES OF THE ORDER FOR GOD'S SAKE"*

Some of the angels gave Absolution a slight nod in agreement. Armin took notice. He could not risk the Angels taking sides against one another. The realms needed protection, and he could not afford squabbling and in-fighting.

Armin sighed and took another deep breath. He knew what he MUST say next, although the words proved challenging to form. He asked the Everlasting for help in silent prayer. Help him be the strong leader he was pledged to be.

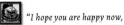 *"Since the tournament was forfeit, so are the lives of tournament participants I am afraid, starting with Absolution's young ward, Percival. He must be put to death by my sword."*

Absolution was petrified, eyes wide open from the events unfolding in front of him. He looked over at Michael, hoping for some sort of reprieve or protection. After all, he protected him for all these centuries, surely, he could do him a small kindness and stop this madness from happening. Michael just stood there, wings flapping in the breeze, unmoved by the look of anguish in Absolution's eyes.

Arms folded, he gave a subtle nod to Armin obey the laws of the Order and begin the ritual.

All the Knights looked dismayed, even alarmed, how could Armin do such a thing? Some Knights began to clutch their weapons as they contemplated a coup; Michael's reassuring nod in agreement with Armin's announcement quenched any further thoughts of rebellion. The Knights looked on in solemn compliance and instructed their scouts to do the same. All except Absolution, who continued to plead his case and beg for mercy.

"Armin, I know we have had our quarrels in the past, but I beg you; please do not do this. This is my responsibility. The boy is innocent. Let me stand for him. I will take the charge. Take my life. You know that would be more satisfying to you anyway."

Armin pondered the thought in his mind. *It would be great to be rid of the nuisance Absolution has become, questioning his leadership at every turn. It is not like I wanted to lead, I was chosen.* Armin quickly dismissed the thought.

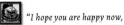 *"I cannot Bane. The rules are clear on this matter. All participants must be put to death. I take no pleasure in this. It must be done. It is the law."*

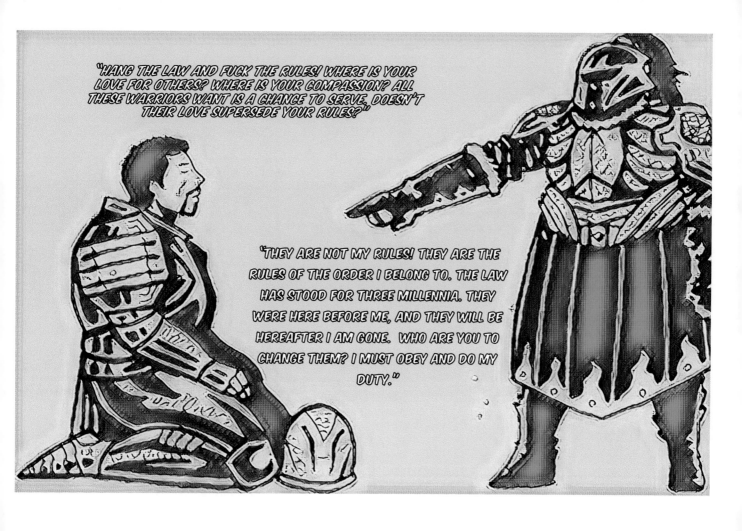

"Gaudfridus, bring Percival to me," Armin requested.

Gaudfridus looked around at his fellow Knights for some type of council or reassuring expression that would not come. He was on his own. Disobey, and he may join the young warrior in death himself. There was no other decision but to do as commanded.

Jewel and Clandor left their seats and exited the realm in disgust; they did not want to be part of such merciless acts.

"Brother...look at me BROTHER"

Absolution pleaded, helm removed to reveal tears streaming down his firm bronze-colored cheeks, begged for mercy. No one had ever seen him without his helmet before or at least since he lost to Armin several centuries ago. Bane was such a hard warrior and companion; it surprised the Order to see such a vulnerable side of him. There was no doubt in their minds that Absolution genuinely cared for his ward.

"Please! Please! You don't have to do this. He is like a son to me! Knights hear me, I know you care for your scouts as well. Don't let this happen! Stand with me!"

He did not get the response he pleaded for. The Knights had gone silent, stone-faced, unwilling to provide aid.

They would not betray their leader nor the code they pledge allegiance to.

Gaudfridus placed the boy on his knees. Percival did not make a fuss. He wanted to make Absolution proud and to go quietly, no whimpering or whining like the warrior legends Bane taught him about.

ARMIN BREATHED IN DEEP AS HE RAISED HIS MASTER SWORD ABOVE HIS HEAD.

ABSOLUTION FUELED WITH REGRET MADE A FEVERED RUSH AT ARMIN; THE ATTEMPT THWARTED BY MICHAEL GRASP.

ARMIN BROUGHT BOTH SWORDS DOWN ACROSS THE NECK WITH SURGICAL PRECISION.

PERCIVAL'S HEAD HIT THE GROUND WITH A THUD AND ROLLED TOWARD BANE. EYES OPEN, THE YOUNG WARD LOOKED AT HIS MENTOR FOR THE FINAL TIME BEFORE HIS SPIRIT LEFT HIS BODY; LEGS AND ARMS STILL JITTERING BEFORE COLLAPSING IN A HEAP ON THE COARSE WHITE SAND.

Michael released his grasp on Absolution

"The deed is done. Bane, please remove the body from the sands, so that we can perform the next execution. Zane, please present your scout, Val-"

Absolution interrupted in a rage. Bane was not ready to simply let things be.

"He was not one of us. He was a scout pretending to be a pledge through your deception and falsehood. This was the only way to cleanse your sins and keep our order pure."

"Pure? You call the murder of an innocent who is without blame...pure! I have had enough of your rules and your order. I denounce the Order and the knights of the Trinity. You are frauds, all of you."

"Why?! Why, would you do this, Armin? Michael? My brothers? Percival was innocent, why kill him for my deception? He was just a boy. I taught him the ways of the knight. He knows the songs, the traditions, the code, he would have been obedient. He would have removed my shame. Percival was my gift to you, a better version of me--and you murdered him because of your prejudice and pride. Hiding behind your rules and your laws doesn't justify taking the life of one of your own!"

Heavy-hearted, but compelled by honor, Armin responded

Armin had enough. The law was the law, and he did what he had to.

"Insolent scout! You will learn to respect your betters! You will learn to respect the law. As the Everlasting is my witness, I banish you from the Third Realm. Leave now or be carried out" Armin spoke on top of his lungs.

Absolution lowered his head and went down to one knee, *"Then do it, for I have nothing left else to lose in this foul land. I raised that child like he was my own, and you and your laws took him from me."*

"They are not my laws; they are the laws of the Order and I must – "

Absolution interrupted again, *"Prove it! Prove that it is Everlasting's law! I spit on the laws of the Order. Will GOD strike me down? Or will he look into my soul and know my cause is just"*

Armin had enough of Bane's boasting and disrespect for all he held sacred. The time for talking had passed.

"If GOD does not kill you for your blasphemy, I will."

ARMIN CHARGED BANE, SWORDS IN BOTH HANDS, READY TO STRIKE WITH MURDEROUS INTENT. BANE DODGED AND COUNTERED WITH A MIGHTY SWING OF HIS WAR HAMMER THAT STRUCK TRUE AND CRUSHED ARMIN'S CHEST PLATE, THE FORCE OF THE BLOW SENT HIM FLYING INTO THE TABERNACLE, SPLITTING IT INTO TWO PIECES.

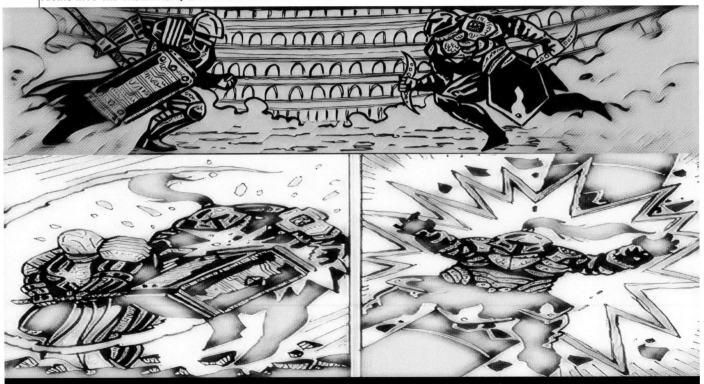

"I didn't say I won't go out without a fight!" Absolution taunted

In shock, Michael rushed over to check on Armin. Armin was a great warrior, but even warriors of his caliber have limits, and the blow delivered by Bane was meant to kill.

The remaining Knights were outraged. Not only had Absolution attacked their leader, but he also had broken the arc tabernacle, a sacred artifact, that had been a symbol of the Order since its inception.

 *"You insult us, and now you betray us,"* Raj pulled out his scepter, *"This cannot stand."*

Absolution was surrounded, escape impossible. The time for prayer and reason was gone, only brutal conflict and the death of the traitor loomed large in their minds.

At Raj's command, the full assault was launched.

"For Percival!"

The war cry reverberated throughout the realms of heaven. Bane's full force was unleashed.

The ground shook violently, dust littered the air--a titanic force, too powerful for the Oracle itself. The impact lifted them off their feet and drove them into the ground below' pieces of the coliseum structure falling all around them. Absolution stood firm, hands trembling; his mighty war hammer reduced to metal shards littered across the white sands.

What happened, he thought to himself as the fog that took over him began to lift. A force like he has never felt before had overtaken him. Something raw and untamed, its fury uncontrollable. Confusion about the power he displayed crowded his thoughts. The sight of his brethren lying in the under the rubble of the Oracle did not help matters. *What did he just do? Was the band of brothers he loved so much, now gone? Killed by his hand?*

The consequences of his actions were too much to bear. Surely, he could no longer be fit for service after this betrayal. The thought brought him to tears.

"Well, you really did it this time, haven't you, Bane? What am I going to do with you?" Michael said compassionately.

The Archangel went to one knee and wiped the tears from Bane's eyes. Absolution took the last look at the destruction he caused, as Michael carried him off in off, far away from the realm he knew and loved.

13 Bane's Charge

""All will pay for the evil they inflict in MY world" – Absolution

EPISODE THIRTEEN
- Absolution learns why the Archangel spared his life all those years ago

Ouch what was that for?"

A bump on the noggin woke Bane from his slumber. The journey to the place between realms was a long one, no matter how fast Michael could fly.

 "You didn't have to slam me on the ground like that."

"Slam you?" questioned Michael. *"Please, you are heavy! All that armor. I keep telling you less is more, Bane. Plus, you could stand to lose a few pounds as well. You are lucky I didn't drop you before we reached this place."*

Bane rubbed his head and surveyed the world around him. This was indeed a place of wonder, topsy-turvy, where time stood still.

WHERE AM I

"Oh, right, I forget that you are not an official member of the Order, hard to believe you have never been here before. This is the place with no name, no man's land if you will. This is where Knights come to travel between worlds."

Bane's eyes flashed with excitement,

"I have always wondered how they did it. I asked Lucis a thousand times, he would never tell me."

"Nor could he. This place cannot be found by someone who is looking for it. It is true, others have encountered this place before, even humans, that is why you see so many abandoned relics with rotting corpses. I can assure they did not mean to find this destination; it is just where they ended up, stranded in-between space and time, poor bastards. No, this is the type of place that finds you. Rest assured, Bane, you are not here

by chance. I brought you here for a reason."

Bane took his eyes off what looked like a floating spaceship turned upside down and refocused his attention toward his master. A rush of emotions overtook him as he reflected on the events that unfolded in the Oracle. He lifted his helm and wiped the tears from his eyes. The mighty order forged by the Divine One himself had fallen, undone by acts of anger, his anger, which must now be judged. Absolution immediately fell to the feet of his master--an act of repentance.

"Forgive me, master, I never meant for it to go so far. How could they kill those scouts, so young and full of holy fire? What kind of Law is that? I think Armin made it up. He made it up just so he could make me suffer for breaking one of his precious rules. The next time I see him, I am going to finish the job and remove his head from his shoulders!"

"Boy, you are a hothead, Bane. Your rage makes you an exceptional warrior but quite a boring conversationalist. Good thing I did not keep you for your manners and charm, eh? Now calm down, your spittle is getting all over me, my feet do not require a shower."

The comment brought a smirk to Bane's face. For all their differences, Michael and his ward always shared the same sense of humor.

"Then why did you keep me? If I am a mean brooding prick, it is because you made me this way! Answer the

question, for once and for all."

Michael let out a sigh, facing these situations too many times. Absolution has always wanted to know why Michael spared him from death so many years ago. After the day Bane had endured, he figured he would indulge him. I mean, it was the least he could do.

"Fine, since I have nothing better to do at the moment, and I don't feel like killing you for getting on my nerves, I will tell you why I spared your life at the Tournament of Heroes so many centuries ago; but I guarantee, you will not like the answer."

 "Try me,"

"Fine"

"YOU WERE SO YOUNG THEN, SUCH A JOYFUL BOY, BUT POWERFUL, WITH A FIGHTING SPIRIT WELL ABOVE YOUR YEARS. WHAT GAVE YOU THE NERVE TO CHALLENGE YOUR OWN MASTER TO A FIGHT TO THE DEATH IS BEYOND ME, BUT THE FACT THAT YOU ALMOST SUCCEEDED, A MARVEL WITHIN ITSELF. WHEN ARMIN DELIVERED THE FINISHING BLOW, I SENSED THE LAST OF YOUR LIGHT GO OUT. EXHAUSTED, YOU FELL TO YOUR KNEES, NEVER GIVING HIM THE SATISFACTION OF SUBMITTAL. THE EMBARRASSMENT IN FRONT OF ALL HIS PEERS INFURIATED ARMIN TO A POINT I HAVE NEVER SEEN HIM BEFORE. ALWAYS THE BOY SCOUT, SO CALM AND CALCULATING, AT THAT POINT, I KNEW THAT HIS VICTORY HAD COST HIM MORE THAN HE WAS WILLING TO ADMIT."

"AS HE RAISED HIS SWORDS TO BRING ME YOUR HEAD, I SENSED SOMETHING IN YOU THAT I HAD NOT WITNESSED IN AN AGE. YOUR LIGHT WAS SPENT, YET YOU HAD ANOTHER FORCE WELLING UP INSIDE OF YOU RAW AND UNTAMED, BUT READY TO BE UNLEASHED. IT WAS SMALL AT THE TIME, BUT I SENSED IT. AT THAT MOMENT, I STAYED ARMIN'S HAND. I TOOK YOU AS MY PERSONAL WARD TO TRAIN—AND AN EXCEPTIONAL STUDENT YOU HAVE BECOME, BESTING EVEN THE TOUGHEST OF DEMONS AND BUILDING A REPUTATION EVEN HIGHER THAN THE ORDER ITSELF. NEVER ONCE HAVE YOU DISAPPOINTED ME OR EVEN TAKEN AN INJURY IN BATTLE, NOT A SINGLE CUT. NOT EVEN OPHILIUS, THE MIGHTY, CAN MAKE THAT CLAIM. I BELIEVE YOU HAVE OBTAINED A POWER RARE TO THE LIKES OF OUR SPECIES, AND OVER TIME, IT HAS GROWN STRONG. JUST AS STRONG AS THE LIGHT IN YOU."

"What are you talking about? I have no powers, remember. For all your training, I am still a scout not worthy of Everlasting's powers given only to the Knights of the Trinity. Breath, Wrath, Fury, Light, Skill, Speed, Dominion, Wisdom, Strength, Divinity, Patience; none of these were granted to me. I use the power of righteousness and GOD's love to vanquish my enemies. As his love is given to us all. That is how I have always won all of my battles with the forces of evil."

Michael nodded in agreement,

"And that is how I have trained you since you were brooding teenager. You have taken my lessons well. However, there is another power inside of you, and from your little episode today, I would say it is reaching its peak."

 "I don't understand,"

"Nor do I expect you to, Bane. Why do you think your strength, your power, surpass those of the chosen twelve? You

are special. I sensed it, and I took you in as my own. The Order would have surely killed you if they knew what I know."*

 "What do you know?! What are you trying to tell me? Stop talking in riddles and just tell me what I want to know, dammit!"

Michael's eyes widened as he felt Bane's unspoken power rising once again. *"You see, there it is! You are using it, and you don't even realize it. Such a simple soul! I grow bored of your stupidity, Bane. Just know that one day you will unleash it, and on the day, all things will change."*

Absolution placed his hands on his head. He was tired of the riddles,

 "What kind of sick, twisted joke is this? I was born an Angel. A being of purity, goodness, and, most importantly, order...how in the hell could I obtain another power outside of the Everlasting's will. Did GOD make a mistake?"

Michael took a deep breath,

"Sigh....again, your ignorance is intolerable. The Everlasting does not make mistakes. He made you special. You are just too dense to see it."

Bane piped up,

 "So why tell me now? I have been asking you for years, and you decide to spill your guts today, there is more to this isn't there?"

"Aww, good boy, there is hope for you yet. Sit with me."

 "As the Archangel, I was the first angel created. Sworn to GODs service, I've witnessed a lot; however, nothing compares to the great divide and the uprising of Lucifer. His lies, treachery, and deception created a civil war with our ranks. It was the worse battle that I have ever been a part of. The dark one killed five of my most loyal knights that day. Using my cunning, I was able to defeat

Lucifer and deliver him to GOD for punishment. An exceptional warrior, I was lucky to overtake him. I waited with great anticipation for the judgment GOD was going to deliver that day. I made it a point to sharpen my sword so that I could take the head of the would-be conqueror. "*

Michael paused for a moment to reflect, then continued,

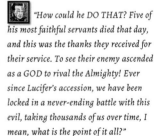 *"And what does the Everlasting decide in his infinite wisdom? Not only does he let Lucifer and his degenerates live, but he also gives the dark one his own kingdom! The smirk on that traitor's face when I delivered him to damnation still haunts me."*

Michael's anger began to rise,

"How could he DO THAT? Five of his most faithful servants died that day, and this was the thanks they received for their service. To see their enemy ascended as a GOD to rival the Almighty! Ever since Lucifer's accession, we have been locked in a never-ending battle with this evil, taking thousands of us over time, I mean, what is the point of it all?"

"Temper, temper, the Everlasting doesn't make mistakes remember?"

Bane said mockingly. The flick of Michael's wrist brought a trickle of blood from Absolutions' mouth.

 "I will not tolerate your insolence, Bane! I am not Armin or one of the other little Knights. You would do well to remember that."

Bane gave a subtle nod of submission.

Michael continued.

 "That was the day I learned the true nature of the will of God, most believe it is all-powerful and reigns supreme with the realms of heaven; but if that is so how was Morningstar able to rebel against it? What did Lucifer possess that I did not, and what would it take to obtain such resistance?"

Absolution interrupted, more puzzled than before

"Stop speaking in riddles. What does this have to do with me?"

 "Ahh, yes, always about you, big baby. Over the past few centuries, I have sensed an uprising approaching, someone or something will try to overthrow GOD's kingdom once again. I am not sure, but I sense that it will have something to do with the realms of man".

Surprised by Michael's revelation, Bane replied, *"The meatbags?! J. C's special little guys. You know I can't stand them".*

 "Yes, I know quite well, Bane, you remind me every chance you get; however since I am banned from setting foot on any man realm for another century, I need you to take Lucis' place as the new protector of Earth. You must succeed where he failed."

Absolution hung his head and breathed deep, *"Lucis was the very best of us. He was the only one who treated me like a brother. How can I ever fill those shoes?"*

 "Yes, Lucis was an exceptional angel and strong warrior, however, his love for mankind blinded him from the truth."

"And what truth is that?"

 "Man has lost their way. It is time for us to see them for the filth they really are, make them atone for their sins against the Everlasting."

Michael put his hand on his ward's shoulder and smiled, *"Now, kneel, Bane. Close your eyes and hold your hands out. I have a surprise for you".*

Bane did as commanded. To his amazement, he opened his eyes to a new Warhammer, freshly forged, and twice the weight of his previous one.

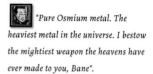 *"Pure Osmium metal. The heaviest metal in the universe. I bestow the mightiest weapon the heavens have ever made to you, Bane".*

"Why me?" asked Absolution voice shaky from the rush of emotion, *"I am lowly scout, not worthy of such an honor."*

Michael replied confidently,

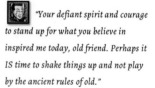 *"Your defiant spirit and courage to stand up for what you believe in inspired me today, old friend. Perhaps it IS time to shake things up and not play by the ancient rules of old."*

Michael slapped him on the back, hard. *"Now, stop with your infernal questions and bow your head!"*

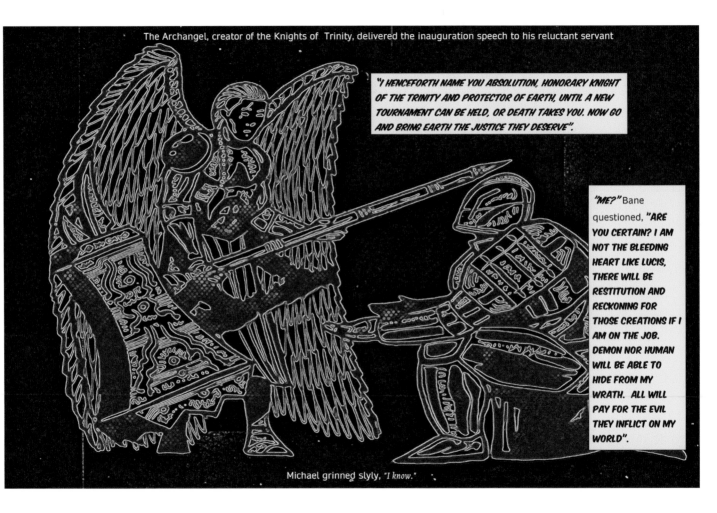

14 | The Seventh Spark

EPISODE FOURTEEN
- A friendly visit turns into an all-out battle for the realm's survival

"Is that the best you can do, foul creatures?" - Clandor

Clandor looked up to the sky

"Is that a star I see? I thought all the stars had fallen, but there you are little fella."

The protector of Thorton folded his tree-trunk arms over his massive chest and chuckled. Standing over 8 feet tall and about half as wide, Clandor was a mountain of man, burly and bare-chested, dark blue complexion with long white hair. He lifted his hands to the heavens, *"Here's to you little star, may the Everlasting bless you to continue to burn bright for the planet you love, just like me"* Being a protector of a realm was a lonely affair. Clandor often held conversations with himself or inanimate objects. These were the only things in which he could reveal his true self without suspicion.

"Hey, star-boy!"

a mysterious figure with a familiar voice bellowed.

"Would you like some company, or are you content to keep talking to that star up there? I think you will find the conversation quite one-sided."

"Galdy? Is that you?" Clandor inquired. Short and stocky, Gaudfridus was half the man Clandor was, literally; but what he lacked in size he gained in vigor and lust for life. Gaudfridus was known to all the knights as the fiery one, quick to action, and even quicker to anger. His grey skin was as thick as an elephant's trunk with long golden hair braided down his back and chin. His golden armor gleamed in the light, which would make a normal man squint and shield his eyes.

But these were not men; they were angels and warrior angels at that.

"None taken, old-timer. If I had a nose as big as yours, I would smell all sorts of things. Come, sit, tell me why you grace me with your presence."

"In the flesh, or in the spirit for that matter. Thank heavens I found you out here in no man's land. I hate disguising myself as a filthy Thortonian. No offense, but your people smell funny."

"Good one, Clandor. I see that years of solitude has loosened you up a bit. This visit might actually be fun."

Tell me, young buck, does Thorton have good ale? I could use a drink or two, or three for that matter! Not that blue-fizzy sludge we chocked down at Artemus' memorial, I had the shits for weeks after that affair"

"Of course, brother, I know just the place. Try and keep up old man."

CLANDOR SHOT INTO THE SKY SO FAST IT LOOKED LIKE A MISSILE. GAUDFRIDUS JUST SMILED AND LAUNCHED HIMSELF AS WELL, DESPERATE TO KEEP UP.

The Conqueror, as he was so fondly known as, was not as fast as he used to be, but there was no way he was going to have some new knight get the better of him. They landed about a mile from a local tavern and took the form of two Thortonian farmers up late from a night of harvesting. Two sat in the back, away from prying eyes or ears for that matter, and began to talk.

 "Well, if you fight as good as you drink, I will agree. Slow down, That is your third glass of Gimlet in under 30 minutes. You are going to make these townsfolk suspicious."

"Fine," Gaudfridus said as chugged another ale, slamming the glass down hard on the table. *"I'll pace myself. No need to cause alarm."*

 "So, tell me, Galdy, what brings you here, you old gargoyle?"

"Ha, gargoyle, eh. I am still young enough to whip your butt, rookie. Besides, nine-hundred and eighty-nine is not THAT old for a warrior."

You are more of a drunk than I remember Clandor thought to himself,

 "So, what do I owe the pleasure of your visit? It has been a decade since we drank together last at Lucis' remembrance ceremony. What has happened in the third realm since then?"

"So, you have not heard. Raj was right."

 "Right about what?"

"THERE IS NO THIRD REALM."

"Bane happened, that is what. I will never forgive him for what he did to us that day!"

 "Okay,"
Clandor said abruptly, placing his hand on top of the cold glass of Gimlet Gaudfridus was trying to consume, *"more talking and less drinking, spit it out already."*

"Well not anymore. It was destroyed the day of the Tournament of Heroes, which we now call the Reckoning."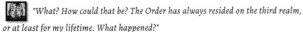

Clandor eyes widened, mouth agape

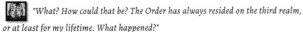 *"What? How could that be? The Order has always resided on the third realm, or at least for my lifetime. What happened?"*

Gaudfridus gave a look of despair and put down his glass. He did not want to relive the day the Third Realm fell, but he needed to tell his young companion--it was the least he could do.

"After you and left, things went bad, real bad. In hindsight, I should have left with you and Jewel, you guys were the smart ones."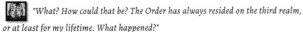

Clandor folded his hands across his chest, waiting for Gaudfridus to get on with it.

"Bane attacked us all, even Armin. He almost killed him."

The Conqueror breathed deep, collecting himself before continuing,

"Before I knew it, weapons were drawn, and an all-out battle for power was in full swing, brother fighting against brother."

"I thought it was just another harmless dust-up, until.... until."

"That was not the worst part"

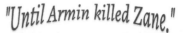 *"Until what? Please get on with it."*

"After our scouts were executed due to Absolutions' lack in judgment, Zane, Stevyn, and a few other knights took sides against Armin and the Order."

Gaudfridus downed another glass of Gimlet and slammed it on the table before continuing.

"Until Armin killed Zane."

Clandor looked at Gaudfridus in shock, totally silent, in disbelief. Gaudfridus continued, tears welling up in his eyes.

> IT WAS AN EPIC BATTLE, DEFINITELY ONE OF LEGEND. TWO MASTER SWORDSMAN GOING HEAD TO HEAD LIKE THAT-- IT WAS A SPECTACLE FOR ALL TO SEE. I DID NOT THINK THEY WOULD TAKE IT SO FAR. ARMIN AT TIMES WOULD TOY WITH ZANE, SEEMING TO STRIKE THE KILLING BLOW BUT WOULD ALWAYS PULL BACK, SMILING AS IF TO SAY, YOU WILL NEVER BE ABLE TO DEFEAT ME. THAT WAS UNTIL ZANE PLUNGED ONE OF HIS SEVEN SWORDS INTO HIS GUT. THE LOOK ON ARMIN'S FACE WAS A SOBERING THING. SO SHOCKED THAT BROTHER WOULD ACTUALLY GO SO FAR TO OVERTHROW HIM. HE HAD NO CHOICE BUT TO CUT ZANE'S THROAT.

> AS SOON AS THE BLOOD HIT THE SACRED SANDS OF THE ORACLE, I KNEW THAT THINGS WOULD NEVER BE THE SAME AGAIN, BUT EVEN I WAS NOT PREPARED FOR WHAT HAPPENED NEXT. THE REALM STARTED TO COLLAPSE WITHIN ITSELF. THE LUSH FOREST AROUND US WITHERED AND DIED. THE FLOWING RIVER AND WATERFALLS DRIED UP. IT WAS CLEAR THAT THE COVENANT WE SHARED WITH THE EVERLASTING HAD BEEN BROKEN. WE KNIGHTS BANDED TOGETHER WITH ONE LAST TO TIME TO ESCAPE DEATH BEFORE IT WAS TOO LATE. UNFORTUNATELY, AZRAEL WAS NOT AS FORTUNATE AS THE REST OF US. FOR ALL HIS STRATEGIES AND SCHEMES, HE COULD NOT PREVENT HIS OWN DEATH.

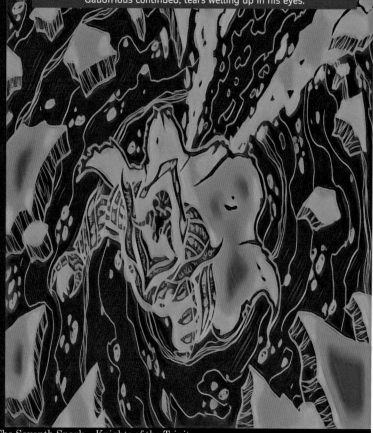

Gaudfridus continued, tears welling up in his eyes.

Gaudfridus looked down at his empty glass.

"Waitress, another round of this fine Gimlet, please. Keep' em coming."

Clandor, anxious to know more, inquired,

 "What happened to the rest of the Order? To you? To the oath, we pledged to protect the realms of men?"

"Oh sure, I am still a barbarian with my great ax; however, I can no longer call upon my divine power, the Wrath of God, defeat my enemies. It makes defeating demons much more strenuous than it used to be, let me tell you."

Gaudfridus paused, took another drink, then inquired,

"How are you getting by without your power, Clandor?"

"The Knights of the Trinity are no more; the Order is divided and leaderless."

"Michael abandoned us after that. No one has seen him or Bane for that matter since that day."

"Worst yet, our POWERS left us as well."

Should I tell him? Clandor pondered. He decided that he would only make things worse. *Besides why make him more miserable than he already is*

 "Well, buddy, I just take it day by day,"

Clandor responded, trying to keep a poker face.

"Well good for you, Clandor. That is the spirit. One day at a time, yes, why didn't I think of that?"

 "So, do you still see them? Any of them?"

 "Well to tell you the truth, I have been too ashamed to show my face"

 "Artemus's shadow looms large, I don't think that I will ever be able to fill his shoes."

 "Look around you, Galdy, what do you see?"

Gaudfridus hung his head and stared into his ale

"Clandor, my boy, you are the first Knight I have seen since that day. We all keep to ourselves now, or at least that is what I would like to believe."

"Enough about me. How are things for you here? Must be hard for a noob, with no guidance from the guild? The fact you never thought to reach out puzzles me."

"Uhh, a bunch of men and women eating and drinking, enjoying life..."

"As well as a bunch of wives and maidens staring at you lustfully, much to their husbands' dismay. Did you have to present such an arousing appearance? Have some humility you show-off."

"You know what I see?" Clandor interrupted, desperate to quell one of Gaudfridus frequent rants,

"I see another person that I have to protect; another sinner doomed for the gates of Hell if I do not keep order and peace on this planet. It is too much responsibility for one being. I am not sure I am cut out for this life."

"I yearn for days past when I could walk the rolling hills of Urien, swim in the Tabor Ocean, and wake up to the three suns of the Orion."

"Those days seem so long ago. Now, when I wake, all I see is forests burning, smoke covering the sunlight, and the stench of dead bodies polluting the oceans. What can I do to stop all the hate and evil that surrounds me?"

"The other day, I saved a kid from dying in the forests of Tullin and brought her back to her family only to find her dead the next day; burned alive by the rebellion."

"Thorton is in the middle of a world war. It is tearing the planet apart, and I feel helpless to stop it."

Gaudfridus looked deep into Clandor's eyes to examine his very soul. The gesture made Clandor even more self-loathing. As Clandor, hung his head low, Gaudfridus let out a roaring laugh so loud that it shook the building at its foundation. The owner of the bar glowered but not dared to disturb these two men from their rousing conversation; after all, it was not a crime to laugh loudly.

Clandor looked up at Gaudfridus's confused response. Gaudfridus waved at the bartender for another ale and continued to make his point to Clandor.

"Boy, tell me something, do you see that lady over there?" Gaudfridus pointed at a pretty lassie over in the corner.

Clandor snickered as Gaudfridus took back control.

"While you were taking a piss, I looked into her soul. That woman's desire was to be a famous singer."

"Over the years, she lost hope and decided to go into prostitution. Of her own free will, she chooses to be fucked by men every single day. How could something so beautiful to do something so filthy for a gold trinket or two."

 "Yes, she's gorgeous. Do you wish to bed her for a night?"

"What? No! for God's sake. You know the law; angels are banned from having relations with humans--you know this. Now stop glowering at her, you dirty-minded fool and listen."

Gaudfridus banged his fist on the counter and broke his glass, ale spilling on the floor. The bartender quickly disposed of the mess and gave Gaudfridus another Gimlet to be drowned in.

 "Brother, why does this bother you so much?"

"It doesn't, at least not anymore. You see, Clandor, I was once like you...well, a little smarter, but I still cared, just like you, I still believed in them."

He raised his glass at the humans of Thorton. The patrons at the bar returned the gesture.

He continued, lowering his voice to avoid suspicion.

"They were doomed from their creation, and here you are weeping for them like poor innocent babies."

"Let me be clear. They are not innocent, and they sure as hell aren't babies."

"You really are as young and foolish as your former master Stevyn said you were."

"I forgot that you've only been Guardian of Thorton for twelve years. You still have ambitions of SAVING mankind?!"

"Ridiculous! Mankind is doomed!"

Clandor rolled his eyes as Gaudfridus' rant continued,

"GOD gave em' the greatest gift of all. The gift of free will."

"For all of our great blessings, we will never control our own destiny or master our own fate--and what have they done with it?"

Clandor signaled to the waiter, perhaps another drink would shut the old geezer up. He continued,

"They introduced sin into the world, cursed their own creator, turned against one another based on skin color and other subtle differences, made weapons of mass destruction, even try to replace GOD by creating artificial life."

Gaudfridus grabbed Clandor by the back of his neck and brought him closer, speaking softly.

"The Everlasting, your creator, your master...knew. He knew there would be sinners in this world, and they needed a special place."

"Let the sinner be doomed for the gates of Hell, for it is their destiny."

And here you are, weeping for mankind the same as you weep for your brothers in arms. Preposterous!"

Gaudfridus paused to take a sip and found his mug filled to the brim. He nodded to the bartender for prompt service, then continued with his alcohol-fueled sermon,

"Foolish boy...why do you think God made Hell? Because he was bored?"

"It's better this way, you know, less of a crowd in heaven! Indeed, the gesture of love for these things, our subjects, these people, is comical."

Shocked by the old-timer's response, Clandor inquired,

 "So how do you do it? How do you keep Planet Zundor safe from destruction?"

"Simple, young one, I don't."

"I accept the fact that my planet is doomed and do what I can to keep their destruction from coming sooner than later. I look for the greatest evil and take pride in its eradication, with the understanding that another ever stronger demonic force will rise up again."

Clandor continued his questioning,

 "How can you do this, knowing that the effort is pointless and that mankind is not worthy of your great axe?"

"That is an easy one, my young friend. I don't do it for them, I do it for the Order."

I know that the fight will never end. I also know that my service ends in my death—and that is the beauty of it all."

"I don't fear it, I embrace it, the never-ending struggle."

"It is what I was ordained to do."

"The Everlasting selected man as his chosen beings, destined to be in his presence for all time. Who am I to deny him? I feel honored that I have a role in making his will come to pass. That is my glory, that is my inspiration."

"Now stop whining like a little baby and pick up the mantle left by the mighty Artemus. He would not be happy with what Thorton has become."

"You have let your compassion for these beings blind you from doing your job. A world-war has broken out for Christ's sake. Time to put out this fire before it gets worse."

"What do you mean?"

"There are seven types of demons, did Stevyn not tell you this? This sounds like work of a chaos demon, and a powerful one at that."

"These demons are the masters of confusion and anarchy. If we put an end to this evil force, perhaps we can put an end to this war before it is too late."

 "I, I don't know how to stop it. Both sides have compelling points, and due to free will, I cannot go and kill the leaders of the two groups now can I?"

"Boy, you really are new to this, aren't you? Of course, you cannot kill the leaders of the rebellion, but you can stop the evil that is behind it."

"We?"

"You will stay and help me, as you did in the old days with your buddy Artemus?"

"Why not?"

"I am already drunk, might as well make myself useful."

"Let's just hope we get to him before another spark is lit. I am not sure how many sparks this planet has left."

"Don't be. I was just as dumb as you when I first started."

"When you have been defending the realms of men for over nine hundred years, you are bound to learn a few things."

 "What is a spark?"

"One lesson at a time, young warrior. Now let's go, don't dottle"

 "Thank you, my brother. I am truly humbled by your wisdom."

"Now, stop showing off your pecks for the ladies, and let's do some good old-fashioned demon hunting!"

Gaudfridus extended his arm to make a pact. Clandor returned the gesture in kind. The two warriors tipped the barkeep and took their leave, to the delight of many husbands clinging to their wives.

Clandor's covered them as they strolled through the brush, his great shield clanking every time a pellet of snow rained down upon them.

HIS LIGHT-HEARTED EXPRESSION QUICKLY TURNED SOLEMN AS TO FORECAST THE IMPENDING DOOM TO COME.

 "What was her name?"

 "What?"

 "The woman you talked about...the songstress...what's her name?"

"Jasmine, I think. Why do you wish to know?"

 "Jasmine. Sounds...kind"
Clandor said clearly distracted by the memory of her beauty as the two gazed up at the sky once again.

"Beautiful night, I never get to see snow on Zundor."

Clandor opened his hand to let the snow fall gently on to it.

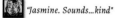

"This is not snow, Galdy, this is..."

Clandor looked up in the dark sky and saw a beam of light coming straight for him and his warrior companion.

The screech of the light echoed over the sky as it barreled toward them at supersonic speed. Using his quick reflexes, Clandor reflected the blast with his shield. The effort caused the beam to ricochet, right into the bar Clandor and Gaudfridus just visited. In an instant, the quaint tavern was reduced to ash and smoke along with the merry patrons inside.

Flesh burning, the fire blazed as the two warriors could only bear witness.

BOOM!

Another blast hit Clandor's shield with exact precision. Clandor held firm. His blessed strength and shield provided him and Gaudfridus all the protection needed to withstand the assault. More beams of light followed all with the same result. Suddenly, the firing stopped, allowing Clandor to cast off his shield and take a breather, even for the briefest of moments.

"What devilry is this?" Clandor inquired, *"That blast was too strong to be man-made."*

"Are you kidding me?" Gaudfridus exclaimed, *"I have no idea. Demons use weapons of old, this is something new, the likes I have never encountered. Oh, What a glorious day."*

That was Gaudfridus, always ready for a fight. The thought of conflict enticed him, another chance to prove his great worth.

A vast entity emerged in the sky the likes the planet Thorton had never seen. Was it a meteorite or a ship? Who could say? The alien vessel covered the sky.

A night of horrors, a chaotic scene. Ashes of the slain thick as billowing smoke. Beams of purple and green firelight rained down, scorching the ground below.

"Hold onto it, keep her steady!"

"That's the plan, Galdy!"

With every strike deflected, colors would fly from his mighty shield. The enchanted scene could be seen by all who gazed upon the sky.

"By god's will, it's like fireworks...fireworks from heaven..." Gaudfridus said in awe of the glorious sight.

Sirens sounded in the distance. The armies of man were

assembling, it would not be long before the Knights were joined by most-welcomed company.

"Finally, I wondered how long it would take for the men of Thorton to get off their assess," Gaudfridus exclaimed.

Aircraft of all shapes and sizes consumed the skies, beyond a reasonable number. The mysterious spaceship was surrounded by Thortian's finest fleet of jet planes and bombers. Clandor held onto his shield, keeping it steady despite the onslaught. Gaudfridus, breathed deeply clutching his golden battle-axe, an axe twice his dwarfed size. *"Remove your shield, and prepare your mighty gauntlets for battle," "Time to show these men what real warriors are capable of."*

The emergency defense system boomed.

"This airspace is restricted...land your vessel immediately or be fired upon. You have 1 minute to comply...."

"You now have 30 seconds to comply...."

"You have 10 sec..."

"You have 10 sec..."

Another blast of epic proportions, the radius wrapped around the sky--twin jets and airships crashed and burst into flames.

In an instant, only the fires and scrap parts remained of the once-mighty fleet.

Clandor and Gaudfridus stood firm, marshaling Thornton's ground forces. Deafening blasts and a few fireworks were nothing new to these warriors of the old guard. A slight tickle to the senses, nothing more. Clandor urged the ground forces

from Thorton to stand behind him. Reluctantly they fell in-line. I mean, it is not every day that you see an 8-foot warrior with golden armor absorbing for all they knew was hellfire. Clandor did his best to inspire them. Men

on his planet were not the most resilient.

"MEN OF THORTON LOOK AT YOUR FATE. YOUR FINEST AIRMEN, SLAIN IN AN INSTANT. SO, WHAT SHALL YOU DO? LOSE HEART AND GO QUIETLY IN THE NIGHT, DOOMED TO DEATH OR SUBMISSION? NO, THAT IS NOT YOUR WAY, IS IT? WE ARE THORTONIANS. A MIGHTY RACE! YES, YOU DON'T KNOW ME, BUT I KNOW YOU. FOR TWELVE YEARS, I HAVE LOOKED OUT FOR YOU, PROTECTED YOU, GUIDED YOU, ALL TO PREVENT THIS DAY. I ASK NOTHING FOR MYSELF, BUT FOR YOU, I ASK THAT YOU PUT ASIDE YOUR PETTY GRIEVANCES AND DIRECT YOUR FURY TOWARD A GREATER EVIL. YOUR SURVIVAL AND MINE DEPEND ON IT. NOT FOR ME, NOT FOR YOU, BUT FOR THORTON!"

Street flooded with soldiers; battle lines formed, with semi-automatic weapons, rocket-launchers, tanks, and other heavy artillery.

"A battle that unites all of Thorton. I bet the chaos demon didn't see this coming. Let's make sure we give these guys what they came for."

"And what is that, Galdy?"

"Hope, my brother. These men follow you because you give them hope. Let's not disappoint them."

"Not to worry, brother, my strength remains" Clandor stood tall, and flexed his muscles for all to see his Herculean strength, *"You forget, youth is gift old man, and I am in my prime."*

The light of the Everlasting emitted from Clandor's aura as he called on his divine power.

"Son of a bitch," Gaudfridus just shook his head in disbelief, *"You lied to me. You didn't lose your power after all."*

CLANDOR GAVE A WINK AS HIS BODY STRETCHED TO TWICE HIS TYPICAL SIZE. A COLOSSUS, FULL GLORY, REVEALED—AN IMPRESSIVE, IMPLAUSIBLE SIGHT. THE MEN OF THORTON GAWKED AT THE SITE IN AWE, THEY QUICKLY RALLIED BEHIND, SUCH STRENGTH, THE FULL ARSENAL AT CLANDOR'S BACK.

THEIR ADVERSARY WAS UNPHASED. A RED AND ORANGE COCKTAIL OF COLORS EMANATED FROM THE SPACECRAFT. A SIGNAL OF SORTS THREE-FINGERED HANDS POPPED OUT OF THE GROUND. HEAD, ABDOMEN, AND FEET SOON TO FOLLOW WITH ASSISTANCE FROM A DRILL ATTACHED TO THEIR THORAX. EQUIPPED WITH PULSE RIFLES, TACTICAL BATTLE SUITS, LASER SWORDS, SHARP CLAWS, AND SERRATED TEETH,

IT WAS CLEAR SOME NEW EVIL NOW SURROUNDED THE THORNTON FORCES THEIR PURPOSE WAS CLEAR, THE ANNIHILATION AND DESTRUCTION OF THE ENTIRE THORTIAN RACE.

THREE-FINGERED HANDS POPPED OUT OF THE GROUND. HEAD, ABDOMEN, AND FEET SOON TO FOLLOW WITH ASSISTANCE FROM A DRILL ATTACHED TO THEIR THORAX. EQUIPPED WITH PULSE RIFLES, TACTICAL BATTLE SUITS, LASER SWORDS, SHARP CLAWS, AND SERRATED TEETH, IT WAS

CLEAR SOME NEW EVIL NOW SURROUNDED THE THORNTON FORCES THEIR PURPOSE WAS CLEAR, THE ANNIHILATION AND DESTRUCTION OF THE ENTIRE THORTIAN RACE.

KREEEEEEET!

With the war cry sounded, the alien horde wasted no time with strategy and launch a full out assault. Their battle tactics were swift, efficient, merciless; they had done this before.

In a matter of hours, Thorton forces were reduced to small squadrons, clinging to what little hope they could afford. As for

Clandor and Gaudfridus, it did not take the beings long to learn to avoid the conflict altogether. Any alien that dared attacked them only offered small amusement, crushed by the weight of their tremendous strength, cunning, and fighting prowess. Sensing defeat, Clandor gave the order

"Gaudfridus, take the remaining Thorton forces to safety, I will do what I can from here."

Gaudfridus fired back,

"Look around you, Clandor! There is no one to save."

The battle for the planet was quickly becoming a massacre. The remains of Thorton soldiers stained the ground, pools of red blood and guts intermingled with small shades of purple that gushed out of their alien adversaries.

Bahroom...Bahroom...Bahroom

Three horn blasts sounded from the ship above. Each one was louder than the last. As fast as the attack started, it stopped. The creatures dove back into the ground below, drills humming and churning at a hectic pace. Was this a retreat, or something more sinister? A chill ran up Clandor's spine. With his far-seeing gaze, he looked up at the rock-ship thousands of feet above him. He faintly noticed a figure in the distance. A glowing purplish-blue entity: one red eye on the top of blue flame with resembled a head of some sort. His magnificent appearance indicated to Clandor that this must be their leader. In its hand was a small weapon no bigger than a Snorkel's tail to his eyes.

This is a snorkel

A sense of doom entered his spirit, *this was not an ordinary weapon* he thought to himself.

A shot fired, a flash of purple and red light so big it blocked out the sky. The sound was ominous as if death itself was approaching from on-high. Clandor saw his impending doom coming closer. He quickly looked back at the planet he loved and raised his shield above his head. He did not know to what end this battle would take him; all he knew was now was not the time for despair.

"Everlasting GOD give me your strength. The strength to protect others and not myself. I offer myself as a sacrifice. Not for glory, not for fame, but for your chosen people."

He glowed with immense power and strength; muscles clenched tightly as the blast hit its mark.

A sonic-boom force of epic proportions reflected against his bronze shield and consumed the land. Buildings crumbled, forests collapsed, the ground split, causing both humans and aliens alike to fall to their deaths, but Clandor and his mighty shield remained unharmed. The force of the blast grew more potent, more intense, yet Clandor and his shield remained. Thousands of Thortonians clamored behind him for protection. He stood defiantly,

body half sunk into the ground, yet he stood. His muscles ached, and every bone in his body was broken, yet he stood. Neither the blast nor the unstoppable force preventing it from hitting its mark would yield. Clandor knew what must be done to save the planet he swore to protect. Clandor thanked GOD in silent prayer, then turned to Gaudfridus, who was already in awe of him and his enormous strength. A strength even the late Artemus would envy.

"Thank you, brother. You showed me my purpose before it was too late. Thorton is yours now, protect her as Artemus would have."

Gaudfridus leaped to stop him, but he was too late; his old age was no match for the reflexes of impetuous youth.

CLANDOR PUSHED THE SHIELD ASIDE AND ALLOWED THE FULL FORCE OF THE BLAST TO HIT HIM DIRECTLY. HE OPENED HIS ARMS WIDE AND TOOK ON THE FULL FORCE OF THE IMPACT WITH HIS MASSIVE CHEST, HIS BODY STILL GLOWING FROM THE IMMENSE POWER HE POSSESSED. HE LOOKED UP AT THE PURPLE BLUE-FLAMED BEING IN THE SKY AND SMILED.

"IS THIS THE BEST YOU CAN DO, FOUL CREATURE!"

The mysterious figure stared down at him in disbelief, beads of red sweat pouring down his brow, a clear sign of the terror, flames shaping its body turning a bright red hue. It was the moment of placidly Clandor needed.

HE BREATHED IN DEEPLY, FILLING HIS LUNGS FOR THE LAST TIME. AS HE EXHALED, HIS FULL POWER WAS UNLEASHED AND THOROUGHLY SPENT. BOTH THE BEAM AND CLANDOR'S BODY WERE EXTINGUISHED, ENGULFED IN BLINDING WHITE LIGHT, SAVING THE REMAINING THORTON AS THEY LOOKED ON IN AWE.

The spectacle they witnessed inspired them. The Thorton forces regrouped more determined united and filled with vengeance. Now was not the time to grieve the fallen warrior; now was not the time to fear the unknown; now was the time to stand. A solemn yet inspired Gaudfridus took the lead and got the remaining forces in battle formation. He looked the lot over with a discerning eye. They were tired, they were scared, but there was something different about them than before. At that moment, he realized that Clandor had done what the legendary Artemus could not. Clandor had united the Thorton factions by giving them the only thing that he could ever give them, LOVE.

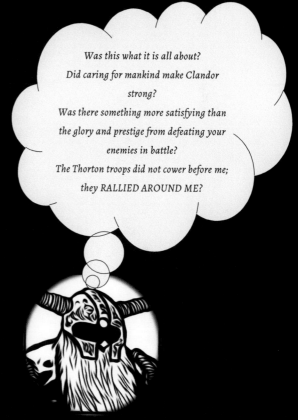

Was this what it is all about?
Did caring for mankind make Clandor strong?
Was there something more satisfying than the glory and prestige from defeating your enemies in battle?
The Thorton troops did not cower before me; they RALLIED AROUND ME?

He always thought of mankind as soft, sinful, weak, yet perhaps, there was something more to them that he never bothered to see before. They are clearly outmatched by a superior race, yet they stand and fight with a fever and conviction that would rival the even the order themselves.

How could he have been so blinded by his own selfish ambitions to not see man for what they truly are, a reflection and testament of GOD's love, just like him? Maybe humans and angels are not so different after all? A single tear fell from his eye as he silently mourned the fallen soldiers of Thorton. Before the lone drop could hit the ground, Gaudfridus felt a familiar tingle shoot down his spine.

A SPARK OF WHITE LIGHT ILLUMINATED FROM HIS FINGERS AND QUICKLY SPREAD. THE POWER OF EVERLASTING, THE ONE HE LOST

A DECADE AGO, WAS RETURNED TO HIM. HE DID NOT KNOW HOW, HE DID NOT KNOW WHY, HE JUST KNEW THAT LOVE FOR MANKIND STIRRED UP IN HIS SPIRIT, LIKE A LONG LOST LOVED ONE COMING HOME. TEARS STREAMED DOWN HIS FACE AS HIS BODY GLOWED A BRILLIANT WHITE LIGHT. GOD'S FURY HAD RETURNED TO HIM, AND HIS WRATH WROUGHT AN INTENSITY AND TERROR THAT NO CREATURE OR BEING COULD WITHSTAND. GAUDFRIDUS RAISED UP HIS MIGHTY GOLDEN AX AND LET OUT A BATTLE CRY SO LOUD IT MADE THE ALIEN ROCK-SHIP SHAKE FROM THE VIBRATIONS.

"For Clandor!"

HE SHOUTED AS THOUSANDS OF THORNTON'S SOLDIERS CHARGED THE ALIEN HORDES IN DEFIANCE; THE BATTLE FOR THORTON WAS JUST BEGINNING...

Closing Remarks

Number One: SPREAD THE WORD

Let people know how much you liked the book, I have ton's
content that I want to release, but content is nothing without
an audience to share it with. So, tell a friend, or two, or three

**Number Two: PICK UP VOLUME TWO OF THE
SEVENTH SPARK – BAND OF BROTHERS**

This book explores the trials of Forge Qaletaga and his beloved
Wrecking Crew as they work to defend the Commonwealth on
Planet Earth. I have included a "sneak peek" of Volume Two on the
next page.

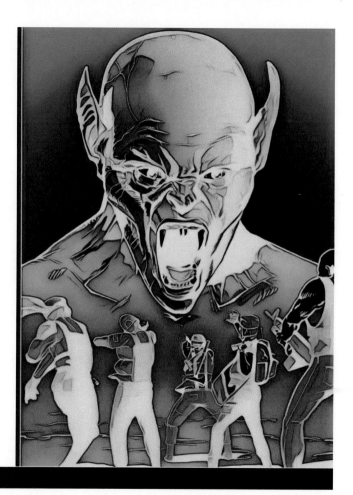

Forge led the way into the darkness that held a thick, choking stench over ground that crunched beneath their boots. When the ground didn't crunch, it squished. No one particularly wanted to lower his light to examine too closely what it was they walked upon.

Losing track of time in the complete darkness of the cavern, they began to bicker.

"Can't see shit in here, and it smells like T. just ripped off another one," DMoney complained.

"Aw, I think Money's scared of the dark," Scorpion's jeer floated through the air. *"Shall I get you a night light?"*

"Whatever, Scorp. When something snatches your tiny ass up, don't ask me for help."

"I can barely see a foot in front of me," Scorpion complained.

"Tell that to Mr. Incredible over there," grumbled Terminator. *"I stumbled over five stones since we entered this godforsaken shithole, and he hasn't missed a beat."*

"Must be that Comanche blood."

"Seriously, somebody better quit touching me," DMoney snarled. *"I'm trying to keep alert, and that shit ain't funny. Bananas, I know it's you."*

"Who, m-m-me?" Bananas snickered.

"Quiet," Forge's voice sliced through their bickering. *"Do you hear that?"*

They listened.

"Someone's coming this way. Follow me."

They followed Forge into a shallow side tunnel.

"Loose the Kraken," Forge whispered.

With a quiet snicker, Bananas extracted his drone and set it free. Light filled the cavern, the drone hovering just out of reach. As their eyes adjusted to the bright light, the crew realized that they were not alone.

Pakistan flag embroidered on his uniform crawled toward them. Beaten, bloody, and with one leg peeled to the bone, he dragged himself across the disgusting cave floor, leaving a trail of blood behind him. When he noticed he was not alone, he began shouting the same thing over and over:

Eurus alshaytanhuna! Eurus alshaytanhuna! Eurus alshaytanhuna!"

Although Forge had no idea what the man was saying, he took solace in knowing he'd found the terrorist soldiers his team had been sent to neutralize. This quest had not been in vain. Like cockroaches, where there was one terrorist, there would be a hundred more hidden from sight. Forge determined that he would explore every inch of that cave if it meant completing his mission and ending al Qaeda's hold on Afghanistan.

"Cap, I know your stance on gratuitous killing, but this guy's going to give away our position," DMoney whispered.

"Permission to use Rod, sir," Terminator offered. *"I'll make it quick."*

Forge nodded. As much blood as the wounded man had lost—dear God, had the flesh being <u>torn</u> from his leg?—he wouldn't live anyway. Why he hadn't already died from blood loss was a mystery that he didn't care to solve.

Terminator pulled out his metal pipe and whispered, *"Okay, boys, time to show you how a man uses his rod."*

DMoney opened his mouth to retort, but a stern glance from his team leader cut off the words.

"Quit clowning around and do the job," Forge snapped. *"If there are any others in here, they'll have heard his screams by now."*

Terminator nodded. *"Yes, Cap."* He approached the man with his pipe raised and said softly, *"Sorry, poor bastard, time to meet your maker."*

The soldier looked up at him.

"What the fuck?" Terminator gasped, and the pipe came crashing down with a dull, sickening crunch. He struck again and again. More blood—always more blood— bits of brain and fragments of skull splattered.

Scorpion lunged forward and grabbed the big man's arm.

"T., what's the matter with you. This bloke was dead four hits ago."

"His eyes! He had no eyes," Terminator babbled, his own eyes wide with uncharacteristic terror, which perturbed his teammates because nothing frightened that man. *"I mean, they were all white, no pupils."*

Printed in Great Britain
by Amazon

Printed in Great Britain
by Amazon